I0553389

Hunted
Blood Hunt: Book 1
Written by
A.J. Marcus
and
Caitlin Ricci

Edited by Cat Lauria

Hunted

Hunted
Copyright © 2017 Caitlin Ricci and A.J. Marcus
Edited by Cat Lauria

Cover art by Caitlin Ricci

ISBN: 978-1-945632-15-0

Published by Mystichawker Press
Look for us online at:
www.mystichawker.com

Chapter One

Malik Converse settled low in the grass, the ground warm against the soft hairs of his stomach as he watched the buck grazing nearby. That deer was the one the pack had to look out for. With his fine set of antlers, he was more than a match for most of the wolves when they hunted solo. The smell of rich earth tickled through Malik's nose as he settled against the ground, waiting for the rest of his hunting party to catch up and close in.

There was an injured doe about five yards from where the buck stood. She definitely hadn't noticed them yet. She was too busy licking at the wound in her leg. Judging by her unwillingness to walk on it, she was probably dealing with something broken. The blood on her fur made Malik think that maybe she'd been in a trap. Whatever had caused her injury, her suffering

Hunted

would be over soon enough and the pack
would have a meal to last them for a week or
two, especially if they stretched her meat in a
stew.

He licked his lips and crawled on his
belly through the grass to get closer to her. If
the hunters had felt like chasing her down
over miles, the way real wolves might have,
then maybe they would have come at her
differently. But they were trying a different
tactic. This was about food more than
anything else, and this hunt needed to happen
quickly, no matter what skills were used for
them to bring the animal down. They had
other packs coming into their territory for the
winter and they needed to have more food to
go around so that they weren't suffering from
the added burden.

Chris Manford, the alpha's son, and
Malik's occasional lover bolted forward
between a few bushes away from him. Malik
charged as well, only he went after another of
the does. She scattered, taking the rest of the
small herd with her. They'd been hoping for
that. Other wolves pushed the deer farther
along as well, getting them well away from

the doe that Chris had managed to separate from the herd. They wanted the group to forget all about her for a little while, just long enough for Chris to deliver the killing blow, as was his right. When his father wasn't around, Chris served in the alpha's role, and they all treated him like the alpha that he would someday be. He was already stronger than most, and none of them doubted he'd be able to best any challenger to the position.

Malik trotted back to their small hunting party and licked the side of Chris's bloody snout. Chris yipped, telling him to eat from the doe as well. He'd already removed the heart for himself and the four hunters laid together around their kill, enjoying the moment. After they fed, they would clean the deer and take the meat back to the pack, but this was their moment to feast and get rewarded for their work before having to share it with the others.

Halfway through their meal, Chris rose to his feet, drawing the attention of the rest of the wolves. When Chris dropped his head and began to growl, Malik jumped up as well, his food forgotten at his feet. He didn't hear or smell anything through the heavy scent of the blood around them, but if Chris must have noticed something, Malik was going to take him seriously. He'd never been wrong about the danger before.

Then, a whole minute after Chris had alerted them, Malik heard what must have set him off. Someone was running toward them. Someone on two legs. Someone much too fast to be human. And someone who reeked of old blood.

Vampire. Malik snarled at the mere thought. They were unnatural and disgusting. They had no business being anywhere near the pack. There had been rumors from other packs of vampires hunting them. So far, the vampires kept their crusade limited to the cities. The Lyons pack didn't venture out of their mountain territory very often, and when they did, they returned quickly.

The rest of the hunters growled softly and eased deep into the shadows of the trees. Malik crawled over to Chris and whined, asking what their hunt leader wanted to do. Chris's gaze darted between the sound of the vampire and the wolves huddled among the trees. In the distance, the deer crashing through the forest still rang out loud and clear.

The sound of the vampire's footfalls had nearly passed by them when they stopped. Silence filled the forest. Not even a breath betrayed the vampire's location. Something beeped.

"Damn," the vampire muttered. There was a rustle of fabric.

Malik held his breath and stayed as still as he possibly could. It was all he could do to stop his tail from twitching.

Another beep.

"What?" the vampire snapped.

There was a pause before a muffled voice replied. The vampire must have put the phone on speaker because Malik could hear both sides of the conversation. "Are you having any luck?" the person on the other end of the call asked.

"I was until your damned call. I'm sure by now these four have scattered."

"What do four werewolves matter? We've got the rest of their pack down. Get your ass over here now. Just follow the fire."

Hunted

Fire! Malik's heart stopped, and he looked over his shoulder toward the pack compound. A bright glow came from the west, and it was long enough since sundown that there shouldn't be any kind of glow there.

At his side, Chris howled before he hurled himself out from cover at the vampire standing there calmly putting his phone back in his pocket.

Malik lunged for Chris, hoping to stop him. Chris was powerful, but he wasn't strong enough to take on a vampire all by himself. He missed, but the other hunters rushed out with him.

The vampire turned on him. He met Chris's attack with one of his own. With blinding speed, he pulled a silver sword from a sheath at his side. The silver flashed in the moonlight for a second before it caught Chris in the back.

Chris yelped and fell to the ground.

The other hunters were on the vampire in a heartbeat. Malik didn't have any choice— he rushed forward as another member of his pack, Wallice, fell to the vampire's blade.

Cheryl managed to get under the vampire's guard and grabbed his wrist. She gave it a sharp twist and the crackling sound of his bones breaking echoed through the forest.

"You're a fast one, aren't you?" The vampire pushed her to the ground.

Malik leaped over her and caught the vampire in the chest, knocking him backward. The blanket of pine needles muffled the sound of their fall. Malik snapped his jaws shut on the vampire's neck and twisted violently.

The vampire's mouth opened like he was about to say something, then he fell silent. His unblinking eyes stared up at the star-filled sky.

Shaking his head, Malik tried to get the vile taste of vampire blood out of his mouth. He staggered off the undead corpse and willed himself to shift. The only true way he knew to make sure a vampire didn't come back from the dead was to take its head.

The silver sword lay a few feet from the vampire. He picked it up.

"What are you doing?" Cheryl asked once she finished shifting.

Hunted

"Making sure the bastard doesn't rise again." Malik lifted the sword and cleaved it down on the vampire's savaged neck as hard as he could. It proved sharp enough to sever the head easily. For good measure, Malik kicked the head to the side, rolling it through years of pine needles.

He'd bent the sword with the force he'd stuck the vampire with. He dropped it and ran to Chris.

Blood pooled around Chris and matted his fur.

Malik dropped to his knees and touched Chris's head. "Try to shift. You might be able to repair some of the damage."

Chris opened his eyes just a crack. There was so much pain in his gaze. He whined and his body shook. The fur on his back and sides rippled as the change started, then Chris yelped and it stopped. Something was very wrong. Chris shuddered and lay still.

"No!" Malik howled as Chris stopped breathing.

The phone in the vampire's pocket started ringing.

Cheryl touched Malik's shoulder. "We

should go. They're going to be looking for us soon. We need to disappear."

Malik growled, but her logic made sense. If they stayed near the bodies, there was a good chance the vampires could find them. They'd lost two hunt members to bring down this one vampire. They had been the strongest warriors the pack had. If there had been more than one vampire, they'd have all perished. He knew better than to try to take on vampires in the middle of the night. Their best chance was going to be finding a place to hole up and then strike at the vampires in the daylight. Strike when they were weak.

"Okay." Malik sighed. "I think I know of a place not far from here." He was about to summon his change when an idea hit him. He went to the vampire and dug into his pockets. He found the thing's wallet and cell phone. Without shifting, Malik turned to run through the forest. "Come on."

"What are you doing?" Cheryl asked again.

"This is information," Malik replied. "We need this. We can shift in a little while after we get somewhere I can leave this for

Hunted

retrieval in the morning." He didn't like the idea of running, but if they were going to have their vengeance against the vampires, they were going to have to make it out alive. They could figure out their next moves when they didn't have vampires hot on their trail.

A.J. Marcus and Caitlin Ricci

Chapter Two

Aren Ibsen frowned in the light of the burning cabins. He was part of Prince...no, he'd called Karl Levy prince for so long, it seemed wrong to call him king, but since the death of his sire, Geb, their previous king, Karl was king of the North American covens. Even the Vampire Council in Europe acknowledged him. There were no vampires strong enough in the states to challenge him and Queen Aleta Montoya, who ruled South America, wasn't speaking out against him— and everyone in power knew how much she hated him.

Since Geb's death at the claws of a werewolf alpha, Karl had been waging a crusade against the werewolves and any other shifters who were stupid enough to show their heads. For the past two months, Karl had led his court on a hunt most every night. They'd managed to eliminate the majority of the werewolves in Colorado and the surrounding states. With Denver being the largest city close to the center of the continent, it was where Karl had decided to set up his court. He'd never liked Geb's city of Saint Louis, claiming it was too humid and too old for a progressive vampire like himself. Aren wasn't sure how a three-thousand-year-old vampire could call himself progressive, but Karl did, and no one was brave enough to call him on it.

As the pack compound burned, Aren wondered if they were going too far in Karl's war with the werewolves. Before Geb's demise, the vampires and werewolves had been uneasy acquaintances at best. But they'd always drawn the line at out-and-out warfare. But their battles were growing so extreme, they might soon attract the attention of the humans. That risked drawing down the Vampire Council on Karl, but Karl didn't seem to care. He was determined to wipe the werewolves out in North America and was trying to talk the European vampires into doing the same.

"Hey, Stephen isn't answering his phone," said Millard Kraus, Karl's right hand, who was coordinating the war.

Aren sighed. The odds were that Stephen

had found the wolves he'd been sent after and was enjoying killing them himself. As a knight of Karl's court, he prided himself on wearing the silver sword and using it as often as he could. For years Stephen had enjoyed using swords, both flesh and steel varieties. His joy in them was obvious and he talked about it often. "I'll go find him."

"Be careful," Karl said as he turned and looked in that direction as well. "This pack was a lot larger than we thought. There may be more than four wolves in the forest, and we may have had some escapees."

"I know how to kill wolves," Aren replied before dashing off in the direction Stephen had gone half an hour earlier.

When he could no longer see the flames of the burning cabins, Aren slowed. It was good to get a decent distance away from the violence. He'd never been a big fan of the turbulent life he led. Unlike a lot of vampires, he preferred his meals willing. Many of the courts liked the ones who struggled against their impending fate, but Aren was one who liked sipping from the same chalice for as long as possible. Unfortunately, there was a

Hunted

limit to the number of times a human could feed a vampire—eventually, even the biggest and strongest of them failed to survive. He'd tried his best to take only as much as he needed, but it was never little enough. Being part of the royal court made it easier for Aren to get the blood he needed, but he still felt each death too personally. He kept hoping he'd find an answer to how to keep going on, and not be weighed down by each meal.

He hadn't been walking long before he caught the smell of blood, a lot of it. Aren listened as hard as he could, but the thick forest was silent, unnaturally so. Even though it didn't sound like there was anyone nearby, he still moved carefully. In the quiet, every one of his footfalls that crunched pine needles made him cringe. If it was that loud for him, then Stephen and the werewolves would be hearing him too.

Aren stepped into a scene of carnage. Two werewolves lay dead. One of the beasts was grotesque. It looked like it had died while shifting from human to wolf, or vice versa. The other one had a long slice on its side, obviously from a silver sword. Stephen lay a few feet away, and his head was missing. The silver sword lay bent across his neck, blood pooling around it. Several feet away, covered in pine needles, Stephen's head lay at an awkward angle as if someone had kicked it there. He wasn't going to be killing any more werewolves, and his gallant flesh sword had seen its last hole.

Pulling out his phone, Aren called Millard. "Stephen's dead. Looks like he killed at least two wolves, but someone chopped his head off with his own sword."

"Dead? That's not possible."

Looking down at Stephen's head, which was already beginning to decompose, Aren scowled. "Sorry, but it is." As he watched, Stephen's blue eyes fell out of their sockets to land on the leaves below.

"Get back here," Millard snapped. "We'll hunt those wolves down later. Karl wants to return to Denver. We just got a summons from the council."

"Be right there." Suddenly wanting to be out of the quiet woods, and not caring if anyone heard his escape, Aren spun on his heels and ran as fast as he could out of the forest. His world was growing darker by the day, and he knew beyond a doubt that he didn't like what was becoming of his life, such as it was.

The main covenstead in Denver was in a state of chaos. The thralls scurried around cleaning and making sure everything was beyond perfect. When the wolf hunters returned, they all stopped and prostrated themselves to the vampires.

The sight irritated Aren. He knew vampires were superior to their food on many levels, but he hated the way Karl made the thralls bow to them. It was wrong. Geb had never done that. In many ways, Geb had been a harsh leader for the North American covens, but he'd never enforced his superiority in such a public manner the way Karl enjoyed doing.

"When will they be here?" Karl barked as they stormed through the front doors. "Where is the original message?"

A blonde female thrall in a black lace negligee rose from the floor. "Juan took the message. He's in the main hall."

Karl didn't pause to acknowledge her. He swept through the entryway and toward the main hall. Aren and the rest of the hunters stayed with him. They were all high enough in the court to know what was going on.

"Where is the message?" Karl shouted as he entered the main hall.

Juan De La Garza, the lowest vampire in the court, turned toward them. "My king." He picked up a piece of paper and came forward since they all knew Karl wasn't about to let any of his court inconvenience him by making him come all the way to them. "Here it is."

Karl took the paper and scanned it before handing it to Aren, who was the closest to him. "Those fools from the old world think they can come over here and catch me with my pants down. I'll show them." He looked at Juan. "Thank you for getting the thralls working so hard before my return. We have much to do."

"Of course, my king." Juan gave him a brief bow. "It is my pleasure to make sure our cattle perform their duties to the best of their ability."

Hunted

Aren bent his head to look at the message, it was the best way to keep Karl from seeing him roll his eyes. It was true that Juan was one of Karl's children, as were a fair number of the lower members of the court, but he hated the way they all groveled to him.

The paper was a printout of an email sent to Karl from Aloren, Vampire King of France and current leader of the Vampire Council. Aren had known Aloren many years ago when they had both been in the French court. He was known to be fair and just—well, as fair and just as any vampire could be. The message said that Aloren and a couple of the other council members would be visiting Denver the next night to see how the newest Vampire King of North America was handling things. The message was short and to the point, with none of the usual pleasantries and flowery language that showed the age of the vampire writing it.

"Aren." Karl walked over to the large plush chair near the fire where he liked to sit.

Not wanting to displease him, Aren hurried after. "Yes, my liege." Aren did his best to not call Karl his king. He had a hard time making the words pass his lips and was always afraid it would sound false, so he chose other terms and hoped Karl wouldn't notice.

"Those wolves who escaped us tonight are the last ones between the Mississippi River and the Continental Divide." Karl steepled his fingers. "With Stephen's unfortunate demise, you are my best huntsman. When the sun sets this evening, I want you to take three others with you and find them."

"My liege, I'm sure I can handle a couple of werewolves on my own." He touched his silver sword.

"They cost me my master of the hunt." Karl frowned. "If we were not having a visit tomorrow, I would send the entire court after them, but alas, I cannot. The four of you must work quickly. Find these wolves and bring them to me." He glanced at the other members of the hunt. "Have we determined which wolf was the alpha of the pack tonight?"

There was a soft murmuring among them

Hunted

before Celeste, Karl's queen, spoke up. "It is impossible to tell, my husband."

"Then we shall display all their heads." Karl clapped his hands. Seconds later a tall, muscular thrall in a thong appeared. "Have two more help you. Go to the trucks and remove the heads of the wolves there. I want them hung around my hall. They will make an appropriate display when the council arrives tomorrow night."

Aren shuddered. It was another thing Geb wouldn't have done. He would've let the wolves burn with their young and their cabins. Karl liked trophies and he always had. It helped stroke his ego.

As the thrall headed out to do as Karl commanded, Aren looked at the other members of the court and tried to decide who to take with him. With the council coming, he'd need to leave most of the higher ranking vampires, but he could take some of the younger ones. They would also be less likely to pick up on how badly he didn't want to be hunting werewolves.

Chapter Three

Malik stretched as he crawled out from under the massive tree roots at the edge of the Little Thompson River. Distance and the river had given him and Cheryl the escape they needed. The sun was barely above the horizon, and he really wished they'd had time for more sleep. He was just thankful he knew of places along the river that were next to impossible to spot and only big enough for two wolves could curl up and hide.

With a slight nudge, Malik woke Cheryl. Her ears drooped and her eyes were bloodshot. He whined softly, then took a few steps to the south, back the way they'd come the previous night. Cheryl heaved a sigh and followed him.

For an hour, they kept to the forest shadows as they went back to their pack lands. They moved slower than they had the previous night when they'd covered the distance in half the time. When they reached pack territory, Malik veered off their previous trail and headed to one of the

23

clothing stashes the pack kept around its lands in case of emergency. The previous times he'd been forced to use the stashes had been few, normally due to a pack member doing something stupid and him needing to be human to get them out of it. He'd dropped the cell phone and wallet in a secluded spot in the base of a tree adjacent to the locker for easy retrieval.

"What are we going to do?" Cheryl asked once she was human again.

Malik shook his head as he opened the storage locker, disguised as a fallen log. "We have to make it back and see how bad it is. We'd better hope the vampires didn't leave any thralls around who might spot us." He pulled out a pair of jeans that would fit him, then some for Cheryl.

Cheryl walked over and looked into the locker. "Why did they do this?"

"I don't know." Malik found a pair of shoes the right size and a shirt that would fit. There weren't many to choose from since most of the men of the pack were close to the same size, or wore extra socks to make the shoes fit if they already didn't. "We've heard rumors, but…" He sighed and shook his head. He couldn't think of any good reason the vampires would be after his kind. For centuries they'd simply avoided each other as much as possible, and it had worked out well for everyone.

"We normally keep our heads down and stay out of their way," Cheryl finished for him. "Maybe it was a stray who pissed one of their court off. But what could one werewolf have done that was so bad that they'd be after all of us now?"

"Maybe we'll find out once we track down that vampire we killed." Malik pulled the shirt over his head. Being clothed felt strangely confining. He wanted to be able to shift at a moment's notice and run if he needed to. The clothes would make that difficult. He'd have continued to run as a wolf into the compound, but if the fire was spotted by the humans, there was likely to be men still there, making sure the blaze didn't spread to the forest. The fact there wasn't a fire raging where they stood was a good indication it hadn't gone far.

"Do you think we can?" Cheryl shook

out her hair after she had her shirt on.

"We'll probably have to go into town and use the computers at the library." Malik had been trying to think of a plan since he woke up. "If the entire compound is a loss, we can hope we at least have a truck to get us to town. Otherwise, it's going to be running while carrying clothes."

Cheryl sighed. "I hate doing that."

"I know." Malik much preferred running unencumbered. Fully clothed, he turned his nose toward the wind and sniffed. The reek of smoke and burned wood surrounded him, making it impossible for him to scent anything else. "Let's go see what they left behind."

On their way to the compound, they found Wallice and Chris, laying as they'd left them, dead on the forest floor. Of the vampire, all that remained was slime-covered clothes with a few bones glistening in the goo. He'd decomposed at an alarming rate. But Malik was just glad he wasn't going to have to get rid of the body. After they made it to the compound and checked it out, they'd come back and bury Chris and Wallice.

"Let's keep moving," Cheryl urged.

Malik didn't say anything, just turned and kept walking toward the life he'd known for many years, a life that had most likely been destroyed the previous night.

Malik and Cheryl stopped at the edge of the trees that ringed the circle of cabins the wolves had called home. The scent of smoke was still strong in the air, and Malik couldn't tell if there were any humans around through it. He didn't see any vehicles, although it looked like there had been a large number of them recently. The ground was soft where lots of water had been used to douse the fires. From their vantage point, it didn't look like any of the cabins had escaped the carnage. A lump formed in his throat.

"This is really awful," Cheryl whispered, her voice breaking in her sadness.

Malik nodded. He knew that he had to be strong and he tried not to let his own fear, or sadness, show. "Let's skirt the edge of the trees. If we don't find any signs of humans, we'll go in."

They kept to the trees as they worked

around the wide clearing the pack had called home. They paused where the road came into the compound to see if they could spot any lingering humans that had chosen to hang around the cabins. There was still no sign of anyone, so they continued on. By the time they made it back to where they had started, Malik was fairly sure they were alone in the forest.

Still staying silent, they walked slowly into the compound. The day before, they wouldn't have taken any precautions when entering the center of the pack's territory. It had been their home. They should've been safe there, but that was before the vampires had come with silver and fire.

Most of the cabins were burned to the foundations. Only their central lodge still had a roof, but it leaned dangerously toward the north where the wall was gone.

"There's no way anyone survived this." Cheryl's voice caught as they slipped into the ruins of the lodge.

"I know. And if any did, the police probably took them to one of the hospitals in Boulder." Malik doubted any of his friends and family were in the hands of humans. The vampires had been too ruthless. He fought to keep his own grief under control. It wouldn't do to lose it. He had to stay focused. They had to find the vampires and take revenge for the destruction of the pack and its lands. There was no way he was going to rest until every vampire responsible for what had been done to their pack met their final death at his claws.

When he and Cheryl had made a complete investigation of the compound, he was ready to leave. Their lives, as they had known them before, were over. The only thing they had left was his old Jeep, that had been parked near the forest and somehow survived the fire that had destroyed everything else. Maybe the vampires hadn't seen it, or maybe they hadn't thought that one old vehicle was important enough to waste their time on.

Malik didn't look back as he drove away from the compound. Maybe one day, when he'd dealt with the vampires, he'd come back and rebuild their pack there. He and Cheryl might be able to find other werewolves to restore the pack with, but they had a lot to do before they could consider that. Like it or not, he had become the alpha.

He drove until they reached the body of the vampire they had killed the night before. He was little more than bones now, his body catching up to his age in his death. "Stay here and keep a look out," Malik told Cheryl as he slipped out of the Jeep. He kept it running in case they needed to make a quick getaway. In the daylight, there wouldn't be any vampires out looking for them, but there could be thralls or curious humans, and Malik didn't have any intention of dealing with either of those groups.

He crouched down next to the skeleton and started going through the pants pockets. Malik didn't much care about this one vampire, but he absolutely wanted to take down the rest of the vampires who had attacked them and he hoped that by finding out more about this one, he and Cheryl could get information about the others, including where they lived. They hadn't taken the time to go through the wallet and cell phone yet— he hoped there would be more than scant, basic information there. Once they got to the library, he'd take time. He felt too exposed and didn't want to risk being interrupted.

"Nothing else that's of any use," Malik called out to Cheryl.

"Good. Hurry up. We've got more work to do."

Malik didn't have to ask what else they had to do. Chris and Wallice needed their attention next. Malik went back to the Jeep, then he began stripping out of his clothes. "We do this as wolves," he said.

Cheryl looked surprised, but she nodded and got out of the Jeep as well.

As soon as he was free of his clothes, Malik shifted and trotted over to Chris's body. Cheryl joined him, and they began to dig.

As a pack, they had buried a few members before. People became old or they fell ill. But Malik had never had to bury someone who had been attacked by vampires. He dug quickly and tried not to think about his grim task, focusing on the soft dirt as he pulled it out of the way. The smell of death became suffocating as they kept going. Malik closed his eyes, but it didn't help keep the scent out. He was the alpha now, and he had to do this for Chris and Wallice, but he hated it. He didn't want to be alpha. He wanted to be back in the field with Chris and the others as they fed on their fresh kill before the vampires had ever arrived.

He was still digging when Cheryl came over and pushed her nose into the thick fur on his neck, silently telling him to stop. They were done. She shifted, letting him stay in the comfort of his fur as she moved Chris's body into the shallow grave. It was a small mercy that she gave him, taking this part of their task away from him. He appreciated it as he sat there at the edge of the grave and watched her place Chris neatly in the dirt. He would never look like he was just sleeping, not with the open wounds across his body, but Malik gave in to the hope that he was at peace.

Cheryl rubbed Malik's head, then she stepped aside, letting him backfill the grave and cover up the son of their former alpha. By the time he was done, she was nearly ready for his help as well. He shifted then silently helped her move Wallice into the grave she'd dug for him. They covered up their fallen pack members together and Malik wished he could inter the rest of his pack as well, but there had been nothing left of them. They couldn't tell if the fire had been so hot as to burn them all to ashes, or if the vampires had taken their bodies for unknown reasons. From the emptiness he felt inside, the secret place where the pack presence had always been, he knew it was only he and Cheryl left.

He wanted to howl and let all of his pain and sadness out into the growing wind, but that wouldn't bring any of them back. Killing the vampires wouldn't accomplish that either, but it would make him feel better.

Cheryl got up first and Malik followed her back to the Jeep. They dressed quickly, and Malik sighed deeply as he got back into the vehicle. "We should go to the library up in Boulder now. There's one right inside the city limits that'll have computers we can use."

He caught Cheryl looking at her nails. His hands were covered in dirt. They couldn't really help that. She gave him a silent nod and he started up the vehicle again. They'd spent hours there and the sun would be setting soon. They'd spent too long already, and they both needed food and water. They had to hurry.

Malik drove as fast as he was comfortable with, which was still well above the speed limit, as he took them into Boulder.

They walked into the library and stopped off in the bathrooms to clean up. Malik let the hot water run over his hands as he stared at himself in the mirror. He didn't look like an alpha. He wasn't ready to be one. He hadn't even been in line to be considered. And, in truth, he didn't have to become the next alpha. He and Cheryl could try to join an existing pack. He didn't have to take up the responsibility of caring for other werewolves. He wasn't built for it like Chris had been. He didn't want to have both of their lives in his hands. He was sure he wouldn't have been any good at it either.

But leaving the territory felt like ditching Chris, and Malik had respected him too much for that. He'd even wanted to love him, once upon a time, when they were reckless teenagers who could have indulged in what they had wanted. Now he knew better, but he wasn't ready to ignore everything Chris had meant to him, or the rest of the pack either for that matter and simply walk away.

No, he had to become the next alpha—he just had to. He had to find it within himself to be an alpha like Chris had planned to be. Someone who cared about every member of the pack and put their wellbeing and safety above his own. He needed to become that person, and that meant he needed to stop burning off his skin with too-hot water and leave the restroom so he and Cheryl could get to work.

He found her waiting for him out in the hallway. "Sorry, I..." He shook his head. He wasn't a child and he couldn't bring himself to say that he'd fallen in. Not today.

Cheryl simply nodded and opened her arms to him. He gratefully stepped into her embrace. "We'll kill them all," Cheryl whispered.

Malik nodded. He knew that they would. She ran her hands through his hair. She was warm and he needed her warmth right then, but when she tried to kiss him Malik pulled away.

Cheryl looked confused, and maybe even a little hurt before her expression cleared. "We are pack, Malik. Giving affection is natural for us. Don't confuse my offer for something more. I know I'm not what you want, and you aren't what I would choose for myself either."

The problem wasn't that he was confusing what she was willing to give him with a relationship, it was that he didn't want any part of that for himself. "Cheryl..." This was neither the time or the place, but she had to know that while he could make himself be her alpha, he couldn't be her mate as well. "We..." He shouldn't have had to explain— the entire pack knew he was gay. They'd all accepted that years ago.

Cheryl rolled her eyes. "I get it. Just stop. We have bigger things to do than worry about you and me. You're my alpha now. I'll follow you anywhere, but that's it. Now, buck up. We're not done yet. We've barely gotten started." She turned away from him with a snap of her hips and he quickly fell in line behind her. As much as he was the alpha now, for better or worse, he was fine letting her take over when it came to finding the information they needed.

Malik stood beside her, keeping watch on the humans around them in case any of them decided to cause trouble. Cheryl borrowed a library card off a kid nearby and used it to get into the computer. He handed her the wallet. She ignored most of it, going straight to the license. She was clumsy as she typed on the keyboard, but Malik knew he would have been no better. They weren't good with technology. No one in the pack had ever been, as far as he knew. Most werewolves resisted change, and technology was change.

It took her around thirty minutes before she got up without a word and walked over to a teenage boy at the desk with a big Help sign above his head. Malik snorted and shook his head as she flirted with the kid until he printed off whatever she had asked him to. Malik met her by the front door as she folded up the paper and stuck it in the front pocket of her jeans.

Hunted

"I have his address and the directions to get us there. We should be at the vampire's front door in two hours. I can drive if you want to rest for a while. Or, we can wait until morning since it's almost dark."

Malik wanted to go after the vampires right that minute, but he wanted to do it safely too. It was just the two of them. He didn't want to do anything stupid that would get them both killed before they could bring the vampires down. "We'll go in the morning. Let's find a cheap place to crash for tonight."

She nodded and drove them to a motel just off the highway, only a few miles outside of Boulder. The rooms smelled like pot smoke, must, and mold, and the beds were lumpy, but they would be safe for the night.

Chapter Four

Aren knelt at the pile of freshly disturbed earth. He knew, without a doubt, that some of the wolves had escaped, and they had come back to bury their dead. Two of them anyway. They'd given their fellow wolves care in death but had left Stephen's body where it lay. It was only bones in clothes too pristine for a body that decomposed to be in. He had a few other vampires collecting Stephen's remains to take back with them to the Council. It was better that he not be left there for the humans to potentially find and start asking questions. In death, things like fangs were more evident.

He'd decided to bring Emory and Daniel along with him on this task. They were both only a few years into their vampire lives and were easy to work with. Neither of them questioned him and they were quick to do as he ordered. There were a few things he liked about being highly ranked in the local court.

Aren turned at the sound of someone coming up behind him. With Emory being so newly made a vampire, he still smelled faintly of the human he'd been. Aren wondered how many vampires had been forced to control themselves around him when he still smelled of rich blood. He was downright intoxicating, and the fact that he was sexy too didn't hurt. But Aren had tried to seduce him months ago, and Emory was far too straight. The odds were that that would change with the years, but he wasn't so pretty Aren would wait for him. There would be others he could be with a lot easier.

His hands shook as he approached and Aren frowned. "Are you cold?"

Emory shook his head. "Nervous, sir. This is the first time anyone on the court has noticed me. I want to make a good impression. Sorry. I'll try better."

Aren rose from the dirt and shook his head. "There's no need for that. You can relax about the formalities while we were out hunting these werewolves. You'll need your energy for going after them far more than you will for wondering how best to appease me. Now, did you have news or were you just interested in having my attention?"

"Daniel found their trail. Two of them, a male and a female, got into a vehicle. They were going west. And it looks like they stripped Stephen of his things. His wallet and phone are gone."

That was very bad news indeed. "Shit." Aren stormed past him and Emory struggled to catch up. "Stephen was always an idiot when it came to his own personal safety. He kept his real address on his license, which'll lead the werewolves straight to the other vampires he lived with." They joined up with Daniel. "Call Stephen's coven, try to reach someone. The werewolves are coming for them and we have to warn them about the danger they're in."

Aren got back into the car they'd driven out in and, as soon as Emory and Daniel were in the car with him, raced out of the forest and back toward the highway. Aren started heading south, toward Stephen's house.

Emory cleared his throat as if deliberately drawing attention to himself. "They might've gone to Boulder."

"Why would they have done that?" Aren snapped as he stared in the rearview mirror.

Hunted

Emory leaned forward from the back seat. "Because they have his address? No werewolf's stupid enough to attack us at night. It's close to midnight now. If they had done anything, we would have heard about it, correct? So I think that they're laying low in Boulder. It's the closest big city."

"He could be right," Daniel added, sounding unsure of himself. Or maybe he was just overly cautious when talking to someone who ranked much higher in Karl's court than he did.

Aren nodded. It was a good idea. It was something he should've thought of, but he was worried enough for Stephen's people he'd overreacted. He did his best to hide his irritation at himself. He headed toward Boulder. "You two, keep a look out. Hopefully, we'll get lucky and find them." Aren spoke casually of killing the werewolves, but in his heart, or whatever was left of it once he had been turned, he wondered at the consequences of what they were doing. Never before had vampires actively hunted werewolves. There had been a few small scuffles here and there throughout the centuries, but since the vampires had moved more into the cities the werewolves had taken up residence in the wilds. There was no reason for them to have come together before and there was certainly no reason for Karl to be starting a war with them.

As he drove, what Karl wanted of them all weighed heavily on him. He was a vampire and feeding was part of that, but killing had never been. He'd done his utter best to avoid it as much as possible, but now, what Karl was demanding of them...this was a slaughter. The pack had members who could have defended themselves and Aren might have been okay attacking them if things had been fair for both sides. But they'd massacred children.

Karl's motto in fighting had always been not to leave anyone alive who could later come back to kill him. That had made sense to Aren as well, up until the night he'd been ordered to attack an unsuspecting village of werewolves. This was not a territory war with other vampires or the need to hunt down a rogue vampire before they could cause trouble and expose the rest of them. This had been murder, and Aren wasn't sure if he was okay with that, regardless of who he'd killed, or who had done the ordering.

"You've known Karl longer than either of us. Are things always like this with him?" Daniel quietly spoke up.

Aren pursed his lips. Speaking ill of their leader was a crime and if anyone found out about it there would be a punishment to fit what they'd done. Aren knew that, and he disagreed with it. No one should blindly follow the commands of their leaders, and yet he had and now people were dead because of his actions. "In some circles, asking that question would get you whipped," Aren chose to remind Daniel.

Emory squeezed himself into the space between the two front seats. "What about in this car?"

They were looking to Aren for advice as their leader, but he wasn't one. He didn't even have a coven of his own—he'd always just moved from court to court, gathering power, but not followers. Karl was who they should have been following, and talking about this was dangerous. Aren swallowed thickly. "I will not turn you in, but I cannot be a part of this conversation either. We've sworn our allegiances to Karl. All of us have, and we must abide by our oaths to obey him in all things." Even if Aren didn't always agree with what Karl said or what he had them do.

Emory and Daniel shared a look.

"We shouldn't say anything," Daniel said. He looked defeated.

Emory nodded. "I don't want to endure another punishment."

That he'd been punished at all was news to Aren. When a vampire misbehaved, he was punished publicly. Always. They were to be made examples out of. "Who punished you?"

"Karl. I refused to bite someone he decided to share with us and I was seen as not being grateful for his generosity. But..." Emory shook his head as he turned to look out the window. "She was crying. I couldn't bite her when she was crying like that. It's so much better when they're willing."

Aren could understand his reluctance

and he also knew about Karl's temper. It was easy to see how things could have easily gotten out of control in that situation. He didn't always need the humans he drank from to be willing, but it helped. When he was young, though, as young as Emory and Daniel, he had cared about that a lot. They weren't far removed from the humans they had been, and so they understandably cared about what the humans felt more than the older vampires. They were more removed from the humans and thought of them as just food.

"It's okay to think like that," Aren said, keeping his voice soft. No one else could hear them, but he was far too used to hiding what he thought around Karl and some of the vampires who thought like him, to start shouting his opinions now.

Daniel looked surprised. "You don't though?"

Aren tightened his hands on the steering wheel as nerves flared to life in his stomach at the dark turn their conversation had taken. "I didn't say that," he replied flatly, hoping his voice gave nothing away.

Glancing in the rearview mirror, he caught Emory staring down at his hands. Then Emory sighed like he wanted to say something but was trying hard not to.

"What?" Aren snapped.

Emory glanced at him, then went back to looking at his hands. "It just doesn't make any sense. Why did the wolves attack us? Why did they kill our king? What could have possibly been their motive? Whatever it was, I highly doubt it was to have vampires going out killing them. It just doesn't make a whole lot of sense."

It didn't make any sense to Aren either, but he tried not to question these things.

Frowning, Emory continued. "I know this isn't popular to voice, and I know I'm a young vampire compared to most at court, so I don't really have a ton of experience, but before I was bitten, I paid a lot of attention to human politics. Things were better under Geb, and I really think Karl is hiding something."

It was Aren's turn to sigh. "Look, saying things like that in most of the community will get you staked. You're a good guy, Emory.

Hunted

Don't screw things up for yourself. I've been in a lot of courts over the years. To be honest, I don't tend to stay in any one too long, because they're all the same. Every few decades something happens and a king is killed. If things go smoothly, the new king won't be that much different than the previous one and everyone is fine for years. Every so often, the new king is a fuck up. When that happens, the Vampire Council swoops in, takes him out and appoints someone else to hold power."

"Do you think that's why the Council is coming?" Daniel asked. "That Karl is fucking up with his crusade to eliminate the werewolves?"

Aren shook his head. He hadn't thought about that. There had been too much going on, particularly with Stephen getting himself killed and them having to hunt down the wolves who did it. But ever since the wolf killed Geb, the entire court had been moving nonstop. None of them had time to think about anything but Karl's next victims.

As they entered the Boulder city limits, Aren's phone rang. He pulled it out and glanced at the screen. Karl. He tapped the phone to answer. "Yes, my liege."

Karl sighed on the other end. "I'm not sure I'm ever going to get tired of hearing my people worship me so." There was a pause. "Have you found the wolves who escaped?"

"Not yet. They left their territory. We're following them now." He stopped for a red light.

"Where are you?"

"Coming into Boulder. It appears they have Stephen's wallet and cell phone. We've warned his coven so they can get to safety. We're going to scour Boulder and see if they have hold up here for the night."

"Boulder." Karl sighed again. "The coven there has been slow to really show their devotion to me. I'll contact their leader and order them to aid us. Oh, Aren, please bring the wolves in alive. I think some amusement for the Council tomorrow night would be good."

As the light changed and he started forward again, Aren cringed. He'd seen what amusement for the Council meant many times. Shifters, particularly werewolves, were a favored entertainment when they had done something to offend vampires, which didn't happen very often. Normally the retribution was limited to one werewolf. Aren secretly hoped the werewolves they were tracking were good at covering their trail and would vanish into the mountains, never to come close to Denver again.

"I will do my best, my liege." Aren didn't really have another safe response.

"I know you will." There was a slight pause. "You know, you've been in the North American court almost as long as I have. I think it's time for you to get a title. Succeed in this and while the representatives of the Council are here, I'll knight you."

Aren had no wish for more rank in Karl's court. He had to control his voice lest something unwanted slip out. "It will be my honor, my liege."

"Yes, it will." Karl ended the call.

"Wow, he's making you a knight?" Daniel said softly. "That's cool."

Aren hoped none of his distaste showed in his expression. "Yes, it is." He would rather endure a cold day in hell than be Karl's knight. The horrors he'd be ordered to perform were things he didn't even want to attempt to imagine.

Two blocks later, his phone rang again. Aren had all the coven leaders in the states on his phone. Karl had thought it was a good idea for his courtiers to be able to reach them if Karl had the need for news to go out quickly. The name of the Boulder coven leader flashed on the phone. Aren answered it quickly.

"Yes, Raul?"

"Our new king has requested my coven assist you in finding some werewolves. Do you know where they are?" Raul sounded bored.

Since Raul was technically beneath him, Aren didn't bother trying to control his irritation. "If I knew where they were, I wouldn't need your help in *finding* them, now would I? There's a good chance they're somewhere in Boulder."

"You don't think they're in Lyons or Loveland? Those areas aren't part of my territory."

"Honestly, I don't know exactly where

they are. They could be in Nederland for all I know. Boulder seems a likely place to start." Aren didn't really want the help of Raul's coven, but since Karl commanded it, there was little he could do about it. "Have your people start looking, sniffing, listening...whatever they're good at. If they get a scent of a werewolf—not a cat shifter, or a feral dog, but a werewolf—then call me and we'll assist in apprehending them. Your coven is not to engage without me there."

Raul yawned. "That's what Karl said too. Where will you be?"

Aren rolled his eyes as he had to stop for yet another red light. "We're starting on the north side of town."

"My people will start at the college and work east. Please let me know when you find something so I can call my coven off the search."

"I will." Aren tapped the phone to end the call. He'd met Raul a number of times since he became the coven leader for Boulder. The vampire was as stoned as most of the people he fed off of and nearly as useless. Aren didn't expect any help from him, or his coven, anytime soon.

It was nearly four in the morning before Aren's phone rang again. He was getting tired of cruising slowly through hotel parking lots and down every street with the windows open in hopes of scenting the werewolves. He'd had to stop and let Daniel and Emory feed, which had required the two younger vampires go into a bar while Aren prowled the area on foot. He was old enough he'd fed two days earlier and would be good for at least another two days unless Karl kept wearing him out.

"We've found something," Raul said after Aren answered the call. "Can't be sure if it's the ones you're looking for, but there's a male and a female werewolf in a motel on the south side of town. We've got their scent down to one room and from the snoring, I'm pretty sure they're asleep."

"Good. Text me the address and wait for us to get there." Aren's pulse sped up. Unless Raul's people were complete incompetents, they could easily subdue two werewolves. He'd really been hoping they wouldn't be

Hunted

found. It would mean more nights of searching until Karl was convinced they'd left the area, but he would've endured that if it meant he didn't have to be part of any more slaughter of innocent wolves.

Chapter Five

The sound of the motel room door shattering jerked Malik awake.

"What?" Cheryl said sleepily.

"Don't let them escape!" someone shouted.

Malik had fallen asleep in his clothes. Something he rarely did, but he hadn't wanted to let his guard down as much as getting undressed would've done. He cursed his stupidity. Clothes made shifting difficult and, as the room was suddenly filled with vampires, he really wanted to run.

Rolling off the bed, Malik tried to put some distance between him and them.

"Oh no, you don't." One of them grabbed his shirt and pulled him up.

Malik hit the vampire as hard as he could. His shirt ripped and he was free as the vampire let out a startled *ooooffff* and slammed against the wall. Malik didn't pause—he willed his hands to change to claws and drove them into the vampire's neck. It wasn't the same as beheading, but he

Hunted

hoped it would at least slow him down.

The vampire crumpled to the floor.

Another leaped at Malik. He raked his claws across that one's face, leaving bone-deep gouges.

Nearby, Cheryl was shouting something he couldn't understand.

A vampire slammed into the wall near Malik. He paused long enough to snap its neck before going on. A strange, raw rage surged up in him. How dare these vampires chase he and Cheryl down. Why were they hunting them in the first place? None of it made any sense, but he had to stay alive. He had to avenge his pack.

Cheryl howled. It wasn't her wolf voice, but her human one. The sound was strange but still carried her anger. She slammed a vampire into the dirty shag carpet before ripping its heart out.

A large, muscled vampire stepped in front of Malik. "The boss says bring you two in alive, but he didn't say how alive." The vampire lunged at Malik.

Malik hit him hard.

The vampire laughed. "I'd heard wolves

are strong. Show me what you got, little doggie."

The rage that had been building in Malik boiled over. He drove his claws deep into the vampire's gut.

The vampire hit him in the head. It was hard enough to make Malik see stars beyond the rage's red haze.

With his hand still in the vampire, Malik tried to find the man's spine in hopes of tearing it out, but all he could feel were soft abdominal tissues.

As the vampire's hands closed around Malik's head, Malik finally found his goal. He clamped his hand around the vampire's backbone and pulled it forward as hard and fast as he could. There was a loud snap and for a split second, Malik wasn't exactly sure if he'd snapped the vampire's spine or the vampire had done him in. Then the vampire collapsed.

"You killed Hans!" a man shouted. Then gunfire erupted.

"No!" someone else yelled.

Malik turned toward the sound.

Cheryl was being dragged off by three

vampires. Another vampire stood in the door to their hotel room firing a pistol at him while yet another flung himself at the shooter.

A bullet caught Malik in the side. He spun and hit the bed as three more shots hit the vampire who was aiming for the shooter.

As soon as the bullet lodged in him, the burning started. *Silver.* Malik knew he wouldn't survive many more shots. Hoping the vampire was a fool, he lay still. Even though they had Cheryl, he had to play dead. He couldn't fight a vampire who had silver bullets. One of the vampires had said they wanted them alive. If they'd leave, he could get the bullet out and go after Cheryl in the daylight. She was pack and he was her alpha. He'd be able to find her no matter where they took her. He wasn't going to lose her on his second day as her alpha. He wouldn't be honoring the position if he did that.

In the distance, sirens wailed. They didn't have much time.

"Get her loaded!" the shooter shouted. "We're done here. One wolf bitch is better than no wolves at all. Karl will be happy."

Then the vampires were gone.

Malik lay there for a couple of minutes, trying to make sure the vampires were really gone before he decided to move. Gritting his teeth, he touched his side where the bullet had entered. His skin was already hot to the touch. He had to act quickly. He had to get the bullet out before the silver spread throughout his system, then he had to get out of the hotel before the sirens reached them. He was thankful the motel had taken cash since he was sure it would have been a lousy idea to use the dead vampire's credit cards. But apparently, that hadn't been enough to keep the vampires from finding them.

Driving his claws into his side, Malik fished out the bullet. His fingers were already slick with vampire blood, and the bullet was deeper than he'd expected. By the time he worked it out, he was sweating and lightheaded.

"I've seen some pretty amazing things in my life, but that has to take the cake," someone said from a couple feet away.

Malik tried to focus his vision on the speaker. It looked like the vampire who dove for the shooter. He growled, but it sounded like something a young pup would make more than a full-grown werewolf.

"I saved your life, wolf," the vampire said. "No need to tear me apart, even if you could in your current state, which I doubt."

Malik tried to shift. It would heal his wound. As soon as he started to, though, the silver in his system flared to life, and pain seared through him. He screamed and clamped his hand over his wounded side as he fell back onto the bed.

"Please, we need to get out of here," pleaded the vampire. "I doubt Raul was smart enough to leave anyone watching, particularly with the human authorities on the way. I could just leave you, but somehow, I think you're important."

After the vampires had destroyed the pack compound the previous night, Malik couldn't believe he was about to trust a vampire, but he didn't see much choice. Until the silver left his system he was going to be weak. If the human authorities took him to the hospital, he'd risk exposing shifter kind to the world.

Baring his teeth, Malik tried to think of something other than the intense pain he was in. "Okay."

The vampire leaned over and started to help him off the bed before groaning and pulling back. "It seems Raul hit me worse than I thought. This isn't going to be easy." He heaved and, with Malik's help, managed to get them both standing.

Being upright made Malik's head swim more, and he clung to the vampire's side. "Where are we going?"

The vampire didn't answer right away as they started stepping over the bodies of the other undead. "I don't know yet," he said finally. He paused at the door and looked back. "I guess it's a good thing most of Raul's coven are young. They won't expose us the way older vampires would."

"We should take them with us," Malik said. There was the unwritten law amongst supernaturals that they never left the bodies of the dead to be discovered by humans. He wouldn't have left the body of the vampire in the forest if it hadn't been decomposing so quickly.

Hunted

"Neither of us has the time or the strength for that." The vampire turned back to the parking lot as red and blue lights began to cast strange patterns across the chipped and flaking paint on the cinderblock walls. "Hang on."

Pain coursed through Malik as the vampire tossed him over his shoulder in a fireman's carry and ran across the parking lot, heading down a dark alley on the other side. When the vampire stumbled, the pain was so bad Malik passed out.

Chapter Six

Aren knew he couldn't call a cab. There would be questions about why he and the werewolf were covered in blood. Other than Raul's place there weren't any coven houses in Boulder. He paused in the alley across from the motel. There were only a few hours before the sun came up. He had to find somewhere safe before then, while at the same time avoiding the human authorities. His chest hurt from the bullets he'd taken. If he still breathed, he'd have been gasping for breath from a collapsed lung. As it was, he was going to need to feed soon to be able to heal the damage Raul had done.

He thought about calling Karl but didn't want to werewolf to fall into his hands. Raul was obviously on his way to Denver, taking the female werewolf to Karl and probably declaring Aren and the male werewolf dead. That wouldn't make Karl happy, but he'd have to honor Raul. Aren was left trying to figure out a way to save both himself and the werewolf from blood loss and sunlight.

Hunted

The neighborhood they were in wasn't one of Boulder's best. Most of the houses, like the motel, were in need of repairs. Aren slipped down the alley as quietly as he could while carrying a muscular werewolf over his shoulder. He listened. Nearby, a man snored. There was a woman coughing. It sounded like there was a lot of fluid in her lungs. Aren paused. The gate to her back yard was open. He slipped in, then eased the werewolf down on the woman's porch steps. The werewolf groaned but didn't cry out.

The woman continued to cough, and Aren tested the back door. It was unlocked. Thankful he didn't have to be invited into the home, he eased the door open, hoping it wouldn't creak as he did. The smell of death lingered in the house. The kitchen was cluttered with unwashed dishes. A fat rat glared at Aren before disappearing behind a bulging bag of garbage. He moved farther into the house. There was only a narrow passageway through most of the place, but the woman's coughing pulled him like a lure pulled a fish.

The main bedroom was less cluttered

than other parts of the house. Aren was actually surprised when he found the woman. Her cough was growing worse. If he had any fear of human diseases, he'd have never considered what he was about to do.

When he touched her shoulder, the woman jerked and stared at him. "Who are-" A rattling cough shook her.

Kneeling next to the bed, he put his finger over her lips. "Do not speak. You are too weak. Are you ready?"

She sighed. "Are you an angel?" she managed to get out in a soft, gasping voice.

Aren nodded slightly. "I am here to take you away from all this. You just need to relax and let go."

A small smile curved her dry, wrinkled lips.

Moving as fast as he could, Aren bent to her aged neck and drained her as quickly as he could.

She gave a breathy sigh as he pulled away, then her heart stopped beating.

"Thank you." Aren crossed her arms and wiped the blood spots from her neck. If there was an investigation into her death, the coroner would have to look really hard to find the evidence of his feeding.

It didn't take him long to find the stairs into the basement. Within minutes he had the werewolf down there, and they were safe from sunlight and discovery.

In the old woman's bathroom, Aren found the supplies he needed to patch the werewolf up. They had less than an hour before sunrise when the werewolf woke up.

"Damn," the werewolf groaned and touched his injured side.

"You're awake." Aren gave him a brief smile. "I was starting to think you wouldn't wake until after sunrise. I hope, if we talk first, you won't kill me in my sleep."

The werewolf glared. "Then you better talk fast."

Aren figured he was going to be a tough sell. "The fact that I saved you doesn't count for anything?"

"Maybe."

"That's a start." Aren offered the werewolf his hand. "My name is Aren Ibsen."

"Malik Converse." He returned the handshake like it was a challenge, and his grip made Aren cringe.

"Malik, it's good to meet you."

"Why are the vampires killing werewolves?" Malik snarled.

Aren wasn't surprised he was cutting right to the case—if their roles were reversed, he'd be doing the same thing. "A werewolf killed our former king. Our new king is trying to make sure those responsible are dead."

Malik shook his head. "That doesn't make any sense. A werewolf would never kill a vampire king. We're not stupid. That would start a war, and we die a lot easier than you all do."

"That's what this is, or at least that's what Karl is treating it as." Admitting that to Malik made the whole thing sound that much worse. Aren suddenly wished he'd left the court when Karl was crowned. It would've been prudent to do so, and very few vampires would've looked down on him for leaving. Many courtiers changed courts when new rulers took charge.

Hunted

"But that's stupid." Malik sat up and leaned against a large box. He grimaced at the movement. "Do you know which pack he belonged to?"

Aren shook his head. "I don't think anyone stopped to ask him, but we knew he couldn't have been working alone. Karl declared all werewolves the enemy."

"Then Karl is an idiot." Malik blinked several times, then closed his eyes.

"I thought you got out the bullet at the motel." Aren hadn't seen any evidence of a bullet still in Malik while he'd been bandaging him.

"I did." Malik opened his eyes and stared at Aren. "But it was in long enough to give me a slight case of silver poisoning. It's going to take my body a few hours to get rid of the toxins in my system."

"You need rest."

Malik nodded. "Where are we?"

"A house I found. The woman who lived here recently died." Aren wasn't sure how much to tell Malik. He had no way of knowing how the wolf would react to hearing the truth of how the woman had died. "We should be safe for the day."

"Good." Malik yawned. "Tell you what. I won't kill you, you don't kill me, and when I wake up I'll go find Cheryl and we'll disappear into the mountains."

"That's going to be harder than you think," Aren said, then he had the flashing thought that Malik might be able to help him stop the werewolf hunts for good. "But if you wait until I wake up, we can work out a plan together. We don't have time now."

"Sunrise coming?"

"Yes. Time is short." Aren didn't know exactly why, but he was fairly sure he was going to be safe with Malik. "We can work out a plan when I wake up."

"Okay." Malik yawned again, then eased back so he was laying on the unfinished basement floor. Within a couple of breaths he was asleep again, but this time it sounded more peaceful than it had earlier.

Aren looked at him in the pale light of the bare, low-wattage light bulb. Malik was ruggedly handsome, someone he would've spent time trying to get close to and win over. Most of his personal thralls had looked a bit

Hunted

like Malik. He liked rugged men who reminded him of the men of his Viking village. If he looked just right, he could see Malik wearing a huge helm and carrying a big ax. That must've been where some of the comfort of having Malik nearby came from.

Chapter Seven

The musty smell of the basement made Malik sneeze. He'd never been a fan of being underground, especially not with a sleeping vampire nearby. He remembered Aren's voice from the night of the fire. He'd called the vampire they'd killed. He'd been there, and even though Malik didn't recognize his scent as having anything to do with what had happened that night, Malik still knew that he'd been there. That made Aren an accomplice if nothing else.

He shook his head and walked upstairs. He needed the distance to be able to think about what his next plan was going to be. As soon as he came onto the main floor, Malik frowned. The smell of death lingered in the air, and it was recent. He followed the scent to where an elderly woman lay. She was clearly dead, and Malik knew without giving the woman a second thought how she had died. He sighed and leaned against the doorway. Aren had killed her. Maybe for her house, maybe to feed. He certainly looked healthier than he had when he'd picked Malik up in the motel. The old woman looked peaceful—there was even a slight smile on her weathered face. She didn't appear to have fought her death.

From the presence of an oxygen machine and the smell of disease about the woman, even before Aren had visited her, she'd been close to death. Malik had always heard that vampires were ruthless savages when it came to feeding on humans. They enjoyed their victims fighting. He could understand that. He enjoyed chasing deer and rabbits in the forest. Getting his own adrenaline up made the hunt that much more exciting. Maybe Aren was different from the stereotypes he'd always heard of. Aren had seemingly honored the old woman with a quick and easy release from the pain she'd been in.

Malik wasn't sure he understood how a vampire who could be part of the slaughter of a pack of werewolves could be so kind to a human. He turned from the bedroom and made his way to the kitchen. Most of the food was quick, easy food—TV dinners and bowls of microwave chili. If the woman had been as sick as Malik surmised, easy meals made sense. He wondered if there was anyone who checked on her daily, or if she had one of those services he'd seen announced on TV that would come by a couple of times a week to get her out and take her shopping or to the doctor. The way the dishes were piled up, he doubted family members checked on her regularly. If that was the case, it could be days before anyone found the woman. Malik didn't like that thought. It wasn't right for the dead to be forgotten like that.

He found a spoon and washed off the remains of what looked like mashed potatoes while he heated a bowl of chili in the microwave. From the smell, there had obviously been more than a few things spilled in there that had never been cleaned up. If he hadn't been so hungry from the silver poisoning, he wasn't sure he'd be able to eat anything that came out of it. But he needed his strength if he was going to rescue Cheryl.

All totaled he heated and ate four bowls of chili, the last in the pantry before he went

Hunted

back downstairs. Somehow it seemed better
for him to stay there, rather than riffle
through the woman's house. She might be
dead, but he didn't want to be nosy. He didn't
care who the woman had been in life. He was
simply in her home until sundown and then
he'd be gone, never to come back.

In the darkness of the basement, he
managed to find the light switch. Aren hadn't
moved. He looked just as dead as the woman
upstairs in her bed. He just didn't smell dead.
He smelled of old blood, but not decay.
Malik realized that was what separated
vampires from animated corpses—they
didn't decompose. The magic that gave them
their unnatural lives made sure they didn't
die until that life was ended. Then their
delayed death caught up with them. That was
why the vampire he'd help kill had been
reduced to bones so quickly.

Malik sat in the spot where he'd slept.
He looked at Aren. The vampire wasn't hard
on the eyes. He was a large man. With his
brown hair and broad shoulders Malik
wondered if he'd been an Eastern European
in life, or maybe he was Scandinavian. Aren

Ibsen could've been a Scandinavian name. His face was a little drawn, but not gaunt. Malik supposed he must stay well fed, and might not have needed to feed off the old woman if he hadn't been injured.

Aren had been injured saving him from more silver bullets. Malik touched his side where the bandages were. He probably wouldn't have survived more than one round. Or if the shooter—he seemed to recall Aren calling him Raul—had been a better shot and actually hit something vital. A gut wound would've killed a human, but his werewolf metabolism was just different enough it didn't do him in. He wanted to know why Aren had dove in front of the gun for him. With vampires hunting werewolves, that didn't make a lot of sense.

Something shifted in the air of the basement. Someone took a breath.

Aren's chest moved ever so slightly. There was a pause and he took another breath. "You're still here." He opened his eyes. Even in the pale light of the bare bulb they were a vivid blue.

"Where else would I have gone?" Malik

Hunted

asked. He kept his voice low. Somehow, it seemed right to do so with the dead woman a floor above them.

"You could've killed me, then gone on a suicide run to save your mate." Aren slowly sat up and ran a long-fingered hand through his hair.

Frowning, Malik shook his head. "She's not my mate. She's my pack sister."

"Oh." Aren shook a bit of dust from his hair. "But you stayed here to watch over me. Thank you."

"You're welcome." Malik inclined his head slightly. "I want to ask you why you saved me."

"Do you want honesty, or what I'm going to plead when we face Karl?"

Malik didn't have time for silly games, even though he suspected vampires were all about games of one form or another. "Honestly, and then you can explain why we're going to face Karl with you pleading."

Aren stood and shook out the long black leather duster he wore. "Right." He fixed Malik with a steely blue stare. "This stays between us. If you mention it to another vampire, I'll deny it and if I have to, I'll kill you. But I really don't want it to come to that."

"Okay, so explain already." Malik stood and wiped the dust from his butt. He really wished he had a clean pair of jeans, but everything but the clothes he'd found in the emergency locker had been burned by the vampires.

"I'm tired of the killing. We've eliminated nearly all the werewolves between the Mississippi River and the Continental Divide." Aren bowed his head and for a moment, Malik thought he was about to dust off his shoes or something. "Karl's war against your kind is wrong. Werewolves don't have a central king like we vampires do. You're all about individual packs and lone wolves. It wasn't some kind of werewolf conspiracy that killed our previous king, Geb—at most, it was one pack. The odds are, we've killed that pack already."

Malik tried to understand. He'd heard the rumors of the vampires hunting his kind, but had no idea the devastation was so widespread. It was a form of genocide. If

Hunted

Aren's king Karl had been responsible for that, Malik had more to avenge than just his pack. He wondered how many wolves had died and if Aren even knew the total count. But he didn't actually want the number. If he knew, it might make him insensible in his grief and he didn't have time for that. He needed to keep moving.

"Is being tired of killing why the old woman upstairs looks so peaceful?" Malik decided he wanted to get off the subject of werewolves, at least for a moment.

Aren glanced at the ceiling as if he could see the bed above them where the woman lay. "She didn't deserve a fight for her life. She was sick and ready to die. I offered her a quick and easy death. I think she welcomed it. She thought I was an angel."

The idea of Aren with a halo made Malik smile despite himself. "I wouldn't say you're that good looking. Maybe devilishly handsome."

"Oh." Aren turned his gaze on Malik. There was a lusty feel to it that made him squirm.

Malik shook his head and ignored Aren's

gaze as best he could. "So what are you going to plead with Karl over?"

"He wanted you and the female alive. I was just trying to fulfill his request. I doubt he was pleased with Raul when he came in with just the female."

"What's going to happen to Cheryl?" Malik wanted to get out of the basement and get to her but knew they needed a plan first.

Aren shrugged. "I don't know exactly what's going to happen. No one said anything about that to me. I just know that the Vampire Council has sent members to check up on Karl and see how he's running his continent. Karl wanted the two of you for tonight's entertainment."

Malik's blood ran cold. "Entertainment? What kind of *entertainment*?" he asked with a growl. He didn't want to think of what vampires thought constituted entertainment.

"Karl's tastes are varied. It's hard to say." He didn't sound like he knew, or even cared. As if what his king did to a werewolf was none of his business. Malik glared at him and tried to rein in his anger. Aren wasn't the enemy, but he was the closest thing to it that

Hunted

Malik had access to at the moment.

Aren walked over to an old dust-covered mirror and rubbed his hands down the front of his shirt. "I wish this didn't have holes in it. It would be easier to get to Denver if we could just call a cab, but neither one of us is in any state for that, unless you happen to know of where we can get some clothes."

"No." Malik shook his head. With the pack gone, he didn't have anyone he could call for help. He'd thrown away the torn T-shirt he'd been wearing since it had just been hanging from one shoulder anyway.

"Let me make a couple of calls and we can sort something out." Aren pulled a phone from his duster pocket.

Malik didn't like trusting the vampire, no matter how sexy he looked in that duster with his rumpled brown hair. But he didn't see any other options. If he was going to rescue Cheryl and pay Karl back for all the wolves he'd killed, Aren was his only option. He just hoped Aren wasn't going to drag him to Karl and give him up as part of the night's festivities.

Chapter Eight

Aren called Daniel. He figured that Daniel would be with Emory and he could reach them both at once.

The call was picked up quickly. "Hey. I'm glad you're okay. We were worried about you."

Aren was surprised that it was Emory who answered the call. He frowned. "I called Daniel."

"He...uh..."

Aren didn't have time for this. "Never mind. What do you know about the female werewolf Raul took?"

"Not much. Just some talk about her being held for after dinner tonight. And someone mentioned a bear shifter too. No one really talks to us about anything. We're with Raul's people now. We considered going back to Karl, but we thought we should wait to hear from you first unless you were really dead. It all got so confusing, with the wolves killing everyone, and then the shooting. Where are you? We can come get you."

Aren glanced over to where Malik stood against the window. He had been looking outside but now he was staring directly at Aren so he'd probably heard. Aren could deal with Malik and his worries later. Right now they needed a ride. "Yes, but only you and Daniel. I have a situation here that Raul can't know about. Are you ready for the address?"

"Yes."

Aren told him where they were, then hung up. "You can relax, Malik. You'll be in good hands with them."

Malik didn't look convinced, and that didn't actually surprise Aren. If their situations were reversed and he was faced with the decision to either trust a couple of werewolves or go in by himself and risk everything he was working for, Aren didn't know which way he would go either.

"How many are coming?" Malik asked. His expression was tight. He was obviously worried about what was to come, even more than he had been moments before.

"Only two. They're young and not very strong, barely more useful than humans."

Aren hoped his words would help calm Malik down, but he only rolled his eyes. "They'll get us to your pack sister."

That seemed to perk up Malik's interest and chase away some of his worries. It was good to have him focused again on what needed to be done, instead of two vampires who wouldn't cause him any harm. "How?"

Aren didn't really have an answer for that. Not yet, at least. First, he needed to talk to Daniel and Emory. "I'm working on that."

Malik glanced out the window again. "Work faster. It seems we've got company." He lifted his lips in a snarl and Aren moved past him to go to the front door.

He checked before opening it to Daniel and Emory. "Inside, quickly. Before someone sees you."

They stopped short just inside of the doorway, and Aren turned around to see Malik blocking their path. He'd expected the werewolf to cower when faced with three vampires, but Malik only looked annoyed. Whether it was at them or at the idea of having to wait a few more minutes for other people to come up with a plan, Aren had no idea, but the annoyance was clear on Malik's face.

"He's a werewolf," Daniel muttered. "The one from the motel who killed most of Raul's coven."

Malik rolled his eyes. "And you bite people to sustain yourself. Now that we have that out of the way, Aren, come up with a plan to get Cheryl free."

"The female werewolf," Aren explained at Emory's confused look. He was sure Emory had plenty of other questions, but they didn't have time for them right now. Thankfully Emory didn't seem too interesting in getting information either, as he simply nodded, accepting they were going to help Malik. "We need to come up with a plan in a hurry. Something that gets the four of us into the covenstead and close enough to be able to get Cheryl free while also not getting us all killed."

"He could pretend to be your plaything," Emory quietly suggested.

Aren's stomach tightened at the idea.

Malik just laughed, until he seemed to realize that no one was laughing along with him. "Oh. You were serious?" Malik looked stunned. "No one would actually believe that, would they? I thought you vampires were above all of the physical pleasure that this world has to offer. I vaguely remember hearing that you all considered yourselves to be ascended or something of that nature."

Malik's information was seriously flawed. Aren decided to quickly educate him. "Some of the older vampires may think like that, but the younger ones certainly still indulge from time to time. Now, as ridiculous as Emory's suggestion is, he's not wrong. We vampires have always had a variety of lovers. A werewolf wouldn't even be the most unusual of them. But to get you in, to make this lie believable, you'd need to lose your attitude when it comes to my kind. You'd have to pretend to want me, to love me almost, all while I treated you as no more than an occasional plaything I decided to bring along for a few days of fun and an easy meal. We'll also need to make this sound like I've kept you hidden for a while. Karl knows I haven't been parading you around in his court."

Hunted

Malik looked between them, and Aren could practically see him making his decision. "How close can you get me to Cheryl if I did this?"

Aren thought hard about it. He wanted to give Malik a best-case scenario, and an honest one at that. "You'd be able to get very close to her. You'd be right with her for part of the night. We vampires, I'm sorry to say, don't really notice your kind when we're not killing you. Who you're with, what you do—as long as you're not being a threat to us in that moment, no one will even look twice at you. Karl wants you all dead, but I've seen vampires have werewolves in their beds as recently as last month. Maybe Karl thinks those werewolves are being controlled and therefore are harmless. We can get you to Cheryl, but getting you out will be trickier."

"And then what? We just help a werewolf, and that's it? We're still there? In Karl's court?" Daniel sounded as if he absolutely hated that idea, but Aren didn't have a better one.

"What would you want instead?" Aren asked. He didn't have time for Daniel and

Emory to get all wishy-washy on him. He needed back up and even though they weren't much, he knew they disagreed with Karl's ideas.

Emory and Daniel shared a look. "If you started your own court we'd follow you."

Malik laughed, drawing their attention.

"What's so funny?" Aren snapped.

"Nothing, really. It's a bit sad actually. My pack is murdered and I'm suddenly the alpha. You're talking about going against the king and these men want you to rule them. I never wanted to be the alpha and from the annoyed expression on your face, I'm guessing you didn't want to be king. Yet here we are, all because your king decided to go after my pack. Is this what irony is? I never quite understood that definition."

Aren waved him away. He didn't have time to deal with Malik's morbid sense of humor. The last thing he wanted to do was think about being king of anything. He'd never been ambitious and enjoyed life in other people's courts. But he would be a better king than Karl. He instantly shook the idea out of his head. "Moving on. I'd have to pretend to be interested in a werewolf and you two would have to pretend to be blindly following Karl's orders just as you always have done."

"It shouldn't be too hard to fake it," Malik said. He stepped closer to them, his voice surprisingly soft given how wary he appeared.

"Pretend to follow Karl's orders? No, I don't think it'll be difficult for us at all," Aren said, only briefly glancing back at him.

Malik came to his side. "I don't care about your king and what you all do about him, as long as the killing of my kind is stopped. What I was referring to is pretending to be your momentary distraction. I don't have to do much, just look enthralled with you. Right?"

Aren assumed that was all that was needed as well. "And you can pull that off?"

Malik nodded. "I think so. I don't have any acting references if that's what you're asking for."

"We might have to kiss," Aren pressed him.

Malik just shrugged him off.

"And if they wonder why you haven't been bitten? Then what?"

"You could have bitten him in a more private spot than his neck or wrist," Daniel offered.

Malik nodded, and Aren was faced with questions about Daniel and Emory that really were none of his business. He'd thought Emory was straight, but he could've been wrong. Or maybe they were just good friends. He quickly moved on from them. "I have my doubts about you being able to pull this off, and if you can't, then it's not just your head that'll be chopped off when they discover our deception."

Malik gave him a hard look before he stepped up against Aren's chest. Aren had no time to react, or even form a thought before Malik had his mouth pressed against him. The kiss was soft, but there was no hesitation or reluctance behind it, at least none Aren could tell. It was simply a kiss, and a good one. But before Aren could begin to enjoy it, or even wrap his arms around Malik, the werewolf was already stepping out of his hold.

Hunted

"I can fake being your lover," Malik said. His words were needless. His little display had made that quite clear. Aren was still watching him as Malik turned to the others. "When can we leave?"

"We'll leave as soon as we're all ready," Aren decided.

Emory nodded, but then his face tightened.

"What is it now?" Aren snapped at him.

"Well, sir, he doesn't really look like a plaything, right? I mean, you've seen them, and he's not...um...he's not dressed for it."

With a sigh of frustration, Aren realized Emory was right. Daniel was blushing uselessly. No matter how good Malik looked in his tight jeans and no shirt, it wasn't a look that would go over well in court. It wasn't subservient enough. "Fine. Go to a pet store and get what he needs. Hurry up, though. We aren't spending all night on this."

They were gone quickly, leaving Aren alone with Malik once again. "What are they getting at a pet store?" Malik asked. His voice gave away nothing, but there was a tightness in his movements that belied how uncomfortable Aren figured he had to be with this whole situation.

Aren leaned against the wall across from him. "Our toys, whether they are humans or shifters, are all to be collared and leashed when around others. I'd forgotten about that. It's been a long time since I bothered to notice who a vampire brought with them. And even longer since I actually had a plaything to drag along to an event."

Malik bared his teeth in a snarl. "It sounds degrading."

"It's the only way to get you through the front door," Aren countered. "And we better hope your pack sister doesn't give you away, or that any of the vampires who were on the hunt when we hit your pack remembers your scent. That could blow everything."

Malik scrunched his face up like he wanted to argue more. Aren expected that. Werewolves were supposed to be rash and unpredictable. But he nodded, subdued. "A few hours of humiliation and then Cheryl and I will disappear. That's not too horrible a price to pay, I suppose. Do you expect me to crawl around as well?"

Hunted

Aren shook his head. "That shouldn't be necessary. Just don't argue with people or look any vampires in the eye. I'll touch you, occasionally, in order to keep up the charade, but I won't do anything more than what will be required to fool them. A kiss here and there, and you've already shown how easy that is to accomplish." He appreciated Malik's decision. It was reasonable of him to do this without making a fuss about it. He knew plenty of young vampires who would have balked at even the suggestion of having to appear to be submissive to another vampire, even for a few hours, and here Malik was, not saying a word against it. He seemed determined to do everything he could to help his friend.

Malik pursed his lips. "It'll be good to start over, but with your king continuing to hunt us down, just leaving doesn't seem like it will solve anything. No werewolf would've killed the previous king for any reason. We generally don't care who runs the vampires as long as we aren't being bothered. But if none of you are going to put a stop to him—and really why would you when he's not killing all of you—then it seems as if the werewolves will need to."

Aren knew he was right, and also that there was no easy solution for their problem either. "Honestly, we're losing a fair number of the younger vampires. The hunts have been hard on them. I think it's the loss of friends that has Daniel and Emory wanting change. It'd be easier for everyone if Karl would just die."

"That can be arranged," Malik smirked.

He couldn't possibly be serious. "No one would let a loose werewolf within a hundred yards of the king. Despite what you might think of us, vampires aren't quite that stupid."

Malik didn't seem to be done with his inane idea yet, though. "Maybe. Maybe not. I've noticed something during my short time around you all, and I've decided that you're pretty arrogant. Maybe you think your attackers are going to be vampires, but you definitely don't think that they're going to be werewolves. You all may believe your previous king was killed by one of my kind, but you still give your back to me and so did Emory and Daniel. I'm just one werewolf, so maybe I'm harmless, but if you can get me alone in the same room as your king then I'll kill him and this can be ended quickly."

His plan may have been a good one, apart from forgetting that Karl wasn't the only vampire who believed that werewolves had killed his father. "There's a slight problem with your plan, though."

Malik looked surprised. "Really? What's that?"

"If you kill our king, then more vampires will go around hunting you in revenge. As long as vampires think that a werewolf killed Geb, then none of you are safe and we'll keep hunting you down." Aren really didn't want to do anything that would keep the fighting going. He wanted to stop the conflict and find a way to make peace with the werewolves. That wasn't going to be possible while Karl was still king, but if Karl wasn't king, they might have options. With the Vampire Council reps in town, anything would be possible. He forced the idea out of his head. Even with Aloren there, Aren wouldn't feel right using his connections to get a position he didn't really want.

Malik's face fell, and Aren knew he understood. Killing one person wasn't going to be the answer. "Do you believe that a werewolf killed your previous king?"

Aren quickly shook his head. He had at first, but the more he thought about it and the more he got to know Malik, the less he believed it. He'd been around long enough to know that just because a leader was spouting something didn't mean it was right. And when he really stopped to think about it, Karl had been *too* loud about the werewolves. Almost like he had something to hide. "It wouldn't make sense for you to and, as much as you've been watching me, I've been watching you as well. You aren't some savage beast who attacks me at every turn, and you're not a feral dog either. Werewolves also don't have the numbers we do, and causing a war would not have helped anyone on your side."

"At least one of you is thinking rationally."

Aren was sure quite a few vampires would agree, but almost none of them would do anything about it. Standing up to the king

Hunted

was dangerous, to say the least, and most of them were comfortable simply falling in line. He doubted if most of the vampires he knew even thought about what they were doing when they went around killing werewolves. It was easy to think of them as simply animals, especially when they didn't look like men all the time.

"Do you think Karl lied then?" Malik crossed his arms and leaned against a wall. It was one of the few places in the living room where there weren't piles of things obstructing passages. The pose made Malik's pecs and biceps stand out.

The look was dangerous, and as he talked, Aren wondered what he would look like with a few leather bands around his arms. They didn't have time to really dress Malik for the part he was about to play, but tight leather pants, or better yet, tight leather shorts would show him off nicely. They were going to have to make do with what Daniel and Emory could find on short notice, and hope no one thought he was slumming when Malik showed up in dirty blue jeans.

"And if he did, what motive would he

have had?" Malik continued, unmindful of Aren's musing.

"Power." It was the easy answer and the first thing that came to Aren's mind. But if Karl was lying about how his father had died, then there had to be a way to expose him. "If you were going to plan to kill a vampire king, how would you do it?"

"I wouldn't."

Suppressing a sigh, Aren rolled his eyes. "Hypothetically."

"Every werewolf knows that the only way to permanently kill one of you is to cut off your head. Then you can't come back." Malik shrugged like it was nothing to him.

Aren touched his throat. "You sound like you've done it before."

"I have. I killed that vampire in the woods with you the night your people attacked my home. I took his sword and I cut off his head." Malik was staring at him now and Aren realized that this was the first time he'd ever been alone with an angry werewolf. Malik looked dangerous, and easily capable of killing any vampire who got in his way.

"Yeah, beheading is the sure way of

Hunted

killing us." Aren was ready for Daniel and Emory to get back so they could hit the road to Denver. He glanced at the plastic cat clock hanging near the front door. It was nearly nine. The stores would be closing, and Karl would be calling his court to dinner. If they were going to rescue Cheryl before the after-dinner entertainment, they needed to hurry. Although, with luck, dinner with Aloren and the other Council reps would be a nice, long drawn out affair, complex as only a bunch of vampires could make it.

Chapter Nine

Malik did his best not to squirm as they drove from Boulder south to Denver. It wasn't a long drive, but being in a car surrounded by vampires wasn't exactly comfortable. The three vampires were a study in contrasts. Aren was obviously the oldest, although he looked to be in his mid-twenties. He had a subtle control and power the other two lacked. If he'd been a wolf, Malik would've figured him for one of the top three or four in the pack. Daniel and Emory, on the other hand, were barely more than pups. They looked to Aren for everything. Seeing them defer to Aren made Malik miss Chris and the way he'd always had the answers the pack needed.

Daniel seemed a lot more taken with Aren than Emory was, who seemed to be trying to figure out what he was doing with his life or lack thereof. From what Malik could tell, Daniel was also more suited to the vampire life than Emory. He wondered if Daniel had sought it out while Emory kind of fell into it. Emory reminded him of a werewolf who'd been bitten and somehow managed to survive. Daniel acted more like someone born to the pack. If they weren't in such dire circumstances, he might've enjoyed watching the two of them more and seeing if he was right.

Daniel drove them to the old money part of town, where the houses were huge estates with sprawling yards and tiny streets running between them. They were close to the zoo, not that Malik had ever been there, but he could smell the animals well enough. Aren pulled up to a driveway that was blocked with a large wrought-iron gate.

A man stuck his head out of the gate house and smiled at them. "Daniel, I thought you were with Raul's coven now. Part of his prize from bringing in the wolf bitch."

"I'm on a special assignment tonight," Daniel replied.

Aren leaned over the seat. "Richard, let us in."

Richard looked surprised. "Aren, Raul told us you were dead."

"No deader than normal." Aren

chuckled.

It made Malik smile too, having a vampire make dead jokes. He liked the fact Aren wasn't completely stuck up, even if he was more than a little bit arrogant.

"I'll call Karl and let him know you're coming in. You're just in time for dinner to be wrapping up." Richard pulled his head back into the guard house and the gate swung open.

"Are we too late?" Malik asked. He couldn't stand it if they ended up being too late to save Cheryl because they'd had to go get him a collar and leash. He wanted to get out of the car and run to her rescue.

Aren shook his head. "Not according to Richard. He might not know everything that's going on in the house, but he's good at keeping track of what's going on around the grounds. If he says dinner isn't over yet, we still have time."

Malik couldn't handle how slowly Daniel was driving up to the front door. He flexed his fingers and willed them not to shift into claws. While he and Aren had been waiting, he'd shifted just to make sure the silver was out of his system. There had been a little more pain than normal, but when he returned to human, the wound on his side had mostly healed and he was ready for a big fight.

Daniel pulled the car up to the end of a long line of cars.

"There are more people here than I expected," Aren said softly.

"That can't be good," Malik observed as a knot formed in his gut. If things went south, at least he and Cheryl would do what they could to take as many vampires with them as possible.

Aren waved off his comment. "It just means a lot of the local coven heads have come to meet the Council reps. It doesn't change our plans. We can make a bigger statement with more witnesses. When Geb was killed, he'd been out in the woods with Karl."

Malik's heart nearly stopped. "Wait a minute, you never told me that. I've seen the way you vampires always do things in groups. Why were they alone in the woods at the time of the attack?" It didn't make any sense at all. If anything it was a perfect setup for Karl to kill Geb and blame the wolves.

"They were family. They occasionally went hunting by themselves. Geb didn't always like the blood the thralls provided. He wanted fresh, off-the-street blood." Aren opened his door and slipped out.

"Stop." Malik hurried after him. "How do you people even know there was a wolf there?"

Aren turned and frowned. "Scent. The same way werewolves track their prey. I was part of the party called in when Karl came back to the house and reported it. Stephen and I went over the area of the park where the attack happened. Karl had scratches." He pulled out the leather leash and snapped it on the ring onto the studded collar around Malik's neck. There was an unreadable look on his face. While the collar was loose, even enough so that he could probably shift without killing himself, Malik still hated the feel of the thing against his neck and the loss of control it implied. "Now Malik, please, for a little while, stop asking questions and pretend to be my plaything. If this goes wrong, it'll be bad for all of us."

Malik shook his head. It made the clip on the leash clink against the D-ring on the collar. "I'll play my role." He ran his hand along Aren's arm, then leaned in to kiss him. It wasn't a bad kiss, even if Aren's lips were a little cooler than the warm werewolf lips he was used to kissing. "I'll be good."

"Thank you." Aren flashed a brief smile, then they followed Daniel and Emory to the door. Getting past the doorman was easy. He was as surprised to see Aren as the gateman had been.

The entryway was immaculate, but there was an underlying scent of fresh blood and it was all Malik could do not to curl his lips and show his teeth. He wanted to trust Aren. So far the vampire hadn't led him wrong, but it went against all of his instincts to walk two paces behind him. But as they moved deeper into the vampire house, and they passed more vampires moving around, he noticed how Aren had been right. Vampires greeted Aren, expressing their thankfulness that he was still alive, but they hardly glanced at Malik. It was if the leash and collar made him invisible to them.

His stomach knotted as the humans among them, mostly scantily dressed, or naked, kept their heads down as if it was forbidden to look at the vampires and guests milling around the house. It didn't take him much to realize these were the thralls he'd heard rumors of, long before he met Aren. They were there as servants and meals for the vampires. It didn't seem right, but he'd heard of humans who were more or fewer vampire groupies and would do anything to be with a vampire. Most probably ended up paying with their lives. As hollow and gaunt as most of the thralls looked, they were near death and welcoming it with open arms.

Daniel and Emory stopped at a large set of open doors.

"Here we go," Daniel murmured.

Aren didn't say anything, he just nodded.

Familiar scents hit him. It smelled like his pack was there, with other wolves. It was all Malik could do to maintain his act and walk calmly beside Aren. He tried to spot where the scent was coming from without stopping and making a spectacle of himself.

Hunted

Doing his best to not look at any of the faces around him, he glanced around. When he spotted the heads on the wall, he stumbled but regained his step quickly. Around the room, trophies hung, most of them human, but there were wolves, and some appeared trapped between wolf and man. He'd wandered into a bigger mess than he'd ever dreamed of. He wanted to run and be safe, but that wasn't an option. He had to play their game out and hope to free Cheryl. Trusting Aren was the only way to do that, but seeing the heads of his packmates on the wall made him more determined than ever to kill Karl.

The room was full of vampires. They were clustered together in little circles, chatting. Each of them had a large brandy snifter in hand. The glasses held various levels of red liquid, and Malik didn't need to guess to know what it was.

From the far end of the room, someone started clapping.

Malik's skin started to crawl as he realized all eyes in the room were on the four of them as they strolled toward the clapper.

He didn't like feeling like prey. He wanted to run and find a safe forest to hide in, but he forced himself to keep walking and not make Aren tighten the leash. The hardest part was keeping his eyes on the floor. He'd remembered as they walked through the door that he wasn't supposed to look any of the vampires in the eyes. It would make it easier to pass under their notice that way. It was also easier to not see the lifeless eyes of his family staring down at him as if urging him to do something.

"Aren, I knew you couldn't be dead," a man said from ahead of them.

"I am sorry that Raul got confused about the state of my health," Aren smoothly said as he stopped a few feet from several large chairs.

"I think Raul gets confused about a large number of things. He said the werewolf had a gun and that he had shot you in the head. I don't see a head wound. And we all know that werewolves don't use guns. Raul isn't invited to this party, but even if he was, I highly doubt he'd notice you. He's not very observant."

Hunted

Malik silently swore that if he survived the night, and if headshot would take out a vampire, he'd go buy the biggest gun he could afford and become a crack shot in no time.

"And, Aren, where did you get this fine werewolf? Have you been keeping him from me?"

"Karl, I've had him for a while now. He's just been in training. He wasn't ready to meet the court. He's rather shy too." Aren pulled on the leash, making Malik step forward. He ran his hand across Malik's chest, sending shivers through him. He stayed calm, despite the raging storm inside his heart. He had to play his role and be good, just as he'd promised.

"You've always liked the passive ones, haven't you?" Karl asked. Malik smirked. He was anything but passive.

"Aren, it's been a long time," another man said.

"Aloren, I'd heard you'd moved up in the world." Aren bowed slightly.

With his head already submissively down, Malik didn't bother copying the move, although Daniel and Emory did. He wondered who the vampire was who commanded such respect from the others.

Aloren chuckled. "Opportunities arise and you seize them, or the world passes you by. Plus, you know how new things help keep old minds more active."

"I do," Aren replied. "We need to sit down and catch up sometime. It's been too long."

Karl shifted his feet. It wasn't clear if he was uncomfortable, or unhappy. "I wasn't aware the two of you knew each other well enough to catch up."

"Aren and I were part of the vampire court of Louis Flambue in France back in the sixteen hundreds. We both floated around the European courts until he decided to go colonial on us and move over here," Aloren said.

Malik stiffened. He'd known Aren was older than he looked—he was a vampire— but over four hundred years was more than he'd been prepared to credit him with.

"That was a long time ago, Aloren," Aren said. "Anyway, I am sorry to have missed dinner, but I'm told there is to be some entertainment tonight."

Karl snickered. "Yes, I suppose most of us have drunk our fill. You know, Aloren, if the Council stays much longer I'm going to have to send out for more thralls. You're going through my supply rather quickly."

"I do apologize." Aloren moved closer to Karl. "One of the hazards of modern travel. It can get expensive to take thralls with us. Ah, for the old days when we could just hit the field and suck down a little shepherd boy."

"Yes, I do tire of having to be so discreet, but luckily Craigslist is a great recruitment tool." Karl paused, then continued in a loud voice. "If everyone would please come out into the back yard, the entertainment portion of the night is about to begin." He touched Aren's arm. "Maybe you would consider adding your new acquisition to the evening."

Aren shook his head. "I don't think so. He's the first one I've found in a long time that I'm thinking about keeping around."

"So your taste are changing a bit," Aloren said as they started walking out of the room. "You were never big into shifters before. I always told you if you let yourself adapt, their blood can be extremely tasty, and they hold up so much better than humans."

Malik fought back a growl. He didn't want to think about letting Aren drink from him. Although their kisses had been nice, he couldn't be subservient to Aren for very long. He was a proud, free werewolf and he was going to stay that way, or die.

"The problem I've always had is they struggle so much. I don't like fighting my food."

"You miss half the fun of it," Karl said.

A slight breeze hit them just before they made it to the back door. Malik caught Cheryl's scent on it. His heart raced. He could smell her fear and agitation and wanted to do what he could to save her. There was also the smell of lilacs and blood wafting around them.

"What are you planning, Karl?" Aren asked. He sounded a bit unsettled. "I figured it would be something in the house."

"With everyone here and it being a beautiful night out, I thought we could be outside." Karl walked across the veranda and stopped near the steps going down into the yard proper. The other vampires filled in around them.

With all the vampires pressing into the space, even though they were outside, it was almost more than Malik could bear. Looking around the yard, he noted that the stone walls were high, but wouldn't be impossible to climb over. If he could get to Cheryl, maybe they could get free of the yard and run before all the vampires had time to react. It wasn't much of a plan, but it was something.

Then he spotted Cheryl being held by two vampires in a square wooden corral halfway across the yard. On the other side of the enclosure, a huge man stood, shaking out his hands and cracking his neck, like a professional fighter would.

Malik's blood ran cold. He recalled Daniel's comment earlier that the entertainment would include a bear shifter. Cheryl wasn't big or strong enough to fight one of them. She'd be torn apart. He really hoped Aren had more plans than he'd let Malik in on. There were too many vampires between Malik and her for him to be able to get through and help out. He couldn't stop his growl of frustration. He wanted to save her and be gone.

Hunted

Chapter Ten

Even though he was in his element, Aren was nervous. There was so much that could go wrong. Karl seemed to be in a very good mood, and or was hiding what he was really feeling so Aloren wouldn't see him upset. One of the first rules of vampire court life was not to let anyone know how you felt. After hundreds of years of dancing the dance of the court, Aren knew who to trust and who not to. He could tell Aloren was hiding something, he just wasn't sure what it was. That made him even more nervous.

Having Malik on a leash behind him gave him a little hope against the vampires massed around them if they decided to attack them. If he made his move and everything went smoothly, their plan just might work. But he was going to need to work quickly. He didn't think Malik would be able to hold it together if the big bear shifter in the ring started ripping Cheryl apart.

"What do you think of him?" Karl asked.

"Him?" Lost in thought, Aren wasn't sure who Karl was talking about.

"The bear." Karl gestured to the fighting ring. "He's the pet of Lady Felicia. When I saw him and knew you and Raul were hunting wolves, I realized a fight would be the perfect way to end the evening."

"Oh. Yes, he's magnificent." Aren replied blandly. The man was large, which Aren preferred, but he had a roughness about him. Like a caged animal ready to kill the minute he was given the command by his master. Aren wasn't a fan of having dangerous men like that in his bed.

"He's bigger than your werewolf at least. If you want, I can pull him aside for you later. I doubt Lady Felicia would mind."

"We'll see," Aren said, hoping his non-answer would be enough to move Karl away from the conversation.

"Walk with me a moment, will you? Your wolf can come along too. He might enjoy this." Karl waved him forward, motioning Aren to follow him. He glanced back and caught Malik watching him too.

"Stay quiet," Aren whispered.

Hunted

Malik gave him a quick nod, then came along behind him. Aren had no idea how he could pull off looking that calm with everything going on around him. Even after being alive for so many years, Aren wasn't sure if he would have been able to pull that off and make it look so easy. He'd gotten tense when they walked into the main audience chamber, but it had probably been the sight of the heads on the wall. Aren wondered who Karl had gotten to mount them so quickly, but it was probably for a show to impress Aloren and the visiting council members. He had no doubt that under other circumstances, Malik would've shredded as many vampires as possible when presented with the heads.

Karl led them to within yards of where Cheryl was being held. "Look at her, Aren. I know you can't appreciate her for what she is, but I do. Or I would like to anyway. You must tell me your secret of how to tame them. She damn near bit me the first time I got close to her."

Malik released a low growl and Aren gave the leash a light tug, warning him to knock it off.

"I find it takes a lot of patience," Aren said as if Malik hadn't growled. "Like I said earlier, I've been working with Malik here for a while. I wanted to make sure he was safe to bring out into polite company. They certainly aren't as easy to control as the humans tend to be. "

Karl chuckled. "No, I don't suppose they are."

While they were alone, or at least as alone as Aren ever hoped to be able to get Karl, he decided to get some information out of him. Karl was obviously distracted by Cheryl so it was possible that Aren might have found a good opening. "I'm sure, if you could, that you would want to tame the one who attacked your father."

"I might do that. I could even thank him for it." He gave Aren a sly smile. "You seem to be ambitious. I'm sure you understand wanting to move up in our ranks. Only, when your father is the king, there aren't many places to go while he's still alive."

Aren understood what Karl was saying, he just couldn't believe everyone had fallen

Hunted

for it, or that he was so openly discussing it
now. Maybe he'd grown too arrogant in his
belief that no one would touch him now that
he was sure he could confess to his father's
murder without any repercussions. "You
know, my wolf said something interesting to
me earlier tonight. He said that if he was
going to kill a vampire, he wouldn't have
scratched him. He would have cut off his
head. I think he's right. That's how I
would've done it too. Only, you weren't
really thinking about that, were you? Was
there ever even a wolf at all?"

Karl laughed. "You *are* smart, Aren. I'll
give you that much. And there was a wolf. A
wild one I stole from the zoo. He wasn't good
for much, but he cast the right scent around.
The problem you have though is there's no
one around to believe your little story."

Aren reached back and deftly unclipped
the leash from Malik's collar. Karl was
right—there were no other high-ranking
vampires in the immediate vicinity—but that
didn't mean Karl was actually safe. "Malik,
get out of here. Now." Aren was glad he
hadn't had to tell Malik twice.

With a few leaps, Malik made it to the fight ring. One of the two vampires holding Cheryl moved to intercept Malik. He grabbed her by the throat and ripped it out with fingers tipped with flashing claws, blood dripping from them.

"Your wolf is foolish," Karl said without looking at Aren. "It seems he wants to be part of the evening's entertainment."

"This evening is nothing if not entertaining," Aren muttered as he grabbed the two ends of the leash. Karl wasn't watching him. If nothing else, Malik was providing him with a perfect distraction.

In the corral, Cheryl dispatched the other vampire holding her and glared at the bear across from her. The bear roared and charged her and Malik.

Aren's chest tightened, almost like his breath was catching, except he didn't have to breathe anymore. He'd wanted Malik to run and be safe. He should've known Malik would save Cheryl regardless of what happened to him.

Malik and Cheryl met the bear's charge and knocked him down to the ground. The bear managed to throw Cheryl across the arena, but she gracefully landed on her feet and ran back toward him as Malik looked more wolfish by the second. He howled. The sound sent a shiver of almost sexual pleasure through Aren.

"If it wasn't two against one, they wouldn't stand a chance," Karl said, a strange eagerness in his voice. "That's the problem with wolves, they don't know how to fight one on one. Without their packs they are nothing."

When Cheryl reached Malik and the bear, something passed between the three of them. Malik straightened and said something just loud enough Aren could hear the sound, but not make out the words. The bear replied similarly, then Malik straightened and offered the bear a hand up. Then the bear and Cheryl leaped the corral fence and disappeared into the trees bordering the yard.

A shout rose from the people on the veranda. Aren had to act quickly. He sensed another old vampire moving toward them.

Karl was distracted for the moment, but it was all the time Aren needed to be able to wrap the leash around Karl's throat and pull it tight. He struggled as Aren moved behind him, forcing Karl to his knees as he held the leash firm between his hands. It wasn't the first time Aren used a garrote; he hated wasting blood. Vampires might not have to breath, but they still needed blood flowing to their brains. Strangulation was slower in the undead than it was in something that required air, but it was still effective. Karl hit his arms and clawed at the leash, but Aren stayed still, ignoring his efforts until finally, Karl went still in his hands.

"You should cut his head off," Malik said from beside him.

Aren glanced over at him. "I told you to leave."

Malik shrugged and undid the leash. "I'm not really all that good at being an obedient pup, and you're not my alpha. Cheryl and the bear are gone. I thought I'd stick around to see how you were going to explain a dead vampire away without blaming us for it."

"I wasn't going to say it was a werewolf," Aren snapped.

Aloren stepped off the path, surprising

them both. Aren hadn't heard him come up at all, and Malik looked just as startled. "I don't think you can blame this one on a werewolf."

Aren bowed his head. He could only hope his past with Aloren would help him survive the night. "I take full responsibility for my actions."

"Good." Aloren chuckled. "Since more than a few of us caught you killing him. It was almost too easy. I think he should've suffered a bit more. I should also thank you."

"For what?" Aren blinked at him, trying to wrap his mind around what was happening.

Aloren sighed and gestured for two of the vampire guards with him to make sure Karl didn't return. "You don't really think the Vampire Council came here just to *check* on him, do you?"

"You've done things like that in the past," Aren replied. He'd seen the Council come swooping in from time to time in every court to make sure things were being done the way they wanted them to be.

"We normally give a king or queen a couple of years before checking up on them."

A.J. Marcus and Caitlin Ricci

Aloren took Aren by the arm as the guards beheaded Karl. "We'd had multiple reports, from both the shifter community and our own people in Karl's court, about his risky behaviors. He was putting us all in danger."

"Wait a minute," Malik said. "You mean you knew, disapproved, and it still took you this long to show up? My pack paid the price for your slowness."

"I am sorry for that," Aloren said. "I think it's time for us to sit down and talk about things. The supernatural community in Europe is changing. Maybe it's time for the community here to change along with it."

Cheryl and the bear interrupted him by coming out of the trees toward them. They both look tired and sweaty.

"Don't any of you know how to stay away from danger?" Aren snapped. He didn't know exactly what was going on, but he really wished someone—anyone—would listen to what he said.

Malik smirked. "Apparently not. What are you two doing back here?"

"Brandon and I want to help. Besides, you're my alpha. Where am I supposed to go

Hunted

without you?" Cheryl huffed.

Malik shrugged and started to take off the collar. Aren let go of Aloren and moved to help him. It was good to see him without the bit of leather around his neck. He ran his fingers around Malik's throat, making sure that the collar hadn't hurt him. The werewolf had a very nice, powerful neck.

"Are you done feeling me up now?"

Aren abruptly dropped his hand. "I wasn't. I was making sure you weren't harmed."

Malik rolled his eyes, but he was smiling. He stepped away as Daniel and Emory came up to them. Their eyes were wide as they looked to Karl's body.

"Stop acting so surprised. Someone was bound to kill him someday," Aren told them. Then he got an idea "Daniel, Emory, please help Aloren's guards take Karl to a suitable dumping ground. He's old enough, he'll be gone by morning. Don't leave anything on him. Malik, you'll stay with me. These two will leave with the body." He waved at the shifters.

"Why am I staying?" Malik asked.

Aren hoped that someday people would simply do what he said instead of asking him so many questions. "For appearances. Losing my werewolf on the same night that the king is killed wouldn't look good. The point of this is to try to stop the slaughter of your kind, not blame you for even more murder. Even though a good number of the court and Council saw me kill Karl, there might be some who won't believe it was justified. I'm trying to keep you safe. Does anyone have any other questions or can we actually get going now?"

No one said anything, so Aren waved them away. Aren looked down at the collar in his hand as Daniel and Emory began to direct the guards to carry the body away. "I need to put this back on you."

Malik shrugged. "I know you do. As long as you know it doesn't mean anything, then I don't mind wearing it."

"It has no significance to me other than a way to keep you safe while we're surrounded by vampires." Everyone else was gone except Aloren. "I hate having you wear it, though."

Malik smiled. "I wouldn't let you put it

on me if you didn't."

Aren looked back to the house and sighed. He really didn't want to go back in, but if they were going to act like everything had gone as planned, they needed to be seen as much as possible.

Aloren touched his arm again. "Come on, Aren, we can't delay things too long. The natives will get restless."

"Fine," Aren sighed and took Aloren's arm. "You're sure I've got the Council's backing on this?"

"Most definitely."

The way he said it made Aren cringe. He realized in those two words, Aloren was going to make him king of North America. It wasn't something that he wanted, but he knew he'd have to take the position. He'd killed Karl, and that made him the most powerful vampire on the continent.

Chapter Eleven

Malik walked silently behind Aren and Aloren as they reentered the house full of vampires. The place was a lot quieter than it had been a few minutes earlier before Aren killed Karl. Some now seemed in awe of Aren, while others were still making small chit chat like nothing had really happened. It made Malik wonder if the vampires could really be as shallow as they appeared.

A woman angrily stormed up to Aren, and Malik lifted his gaze just enough to glance at her before he went back to looking at the floor like a good little vampire's plaything. Thinking of himself like that made him smirk. It wasn't true, and Aren didn't think of him like that either. It was almost amusing to him to be able to fool all of the vampires, who kept smiling and pointing at him as if they were so high and mighty.

"Lady Felicia, what's wrong? You're upset." Aren's voice held a note of amusement.

Malik had to bite back hard on his smile.

Hunted

He was fairly sure this vampire was the one who'd brought the bear to the party.

"Somehow my bear got loose, and he ran away with that wolf. I stepped in for another drink and when I came back, he wasn't in the corral where I left him. Have you seen Karl? I demand to know how this happened. He assured me I wouldn't have to worry about his security and now this. If you see that slimy bastard, you let him know that I'm searching for him."

Aren nodded. "Of course. It's a shame when our toys go missing."

Aloren cleared his throat. "Felicia, I'm afraid Karl won't be around anymore. The issue we came here to address has been dealt with. I am sorry Brandon has taken off. Perhaps if we would all treat our toys a little better, they'd be around longer."

Malik caught her watching him and held still, trying to appear as unassuming as possible.

She quickly seemed to lose interest as she turned away from him again. "True. Do try to have a good a night."

"You too."

"We're going to need to make an announcement," Aloren said.

Aren rolled his eyes. "Must we do it tonight?"

Aloren frowned thoughtfully. "Tell you what, I can make an initial announcement tonight. You go recover from the trauma of killing your king, and we'll talk tomorrow."

"Okay." Aren nodded. "I suppose that will work." He started to walk away, then he turned. "I don't suppose I could run from you?"

"No." Aloren shook his head. "I would track you down personally. I have my own wolves now and they might not know this area, but they could find the two of you without too much problem."

"Fine." Aren snapped and pulled Malik along as he stormed out of the room.

Aren led him toward the front of the house, and then out of it. Malik breathed a little more easily the farther they got from the house. "Where are we going?"

"I was going to call for a ride and get us out of here. Daniel sent me a text—they're all safe at his house and I plan to have them move to mine tomorrow night. My plan for tonight, though, is to get back to my house. You're welcome to stay with me if you want to." He paused and looked back at the covenstead. "I think I'm going to end up living here. I've never been good with big houses."

Malik pursed his lips and, since they seemed to be a good distance from the house, began undoing the collar. He felt a lot better once he was free of it. "You just murdered someone," he reminded Aren.

"I'm a vampire. It's not unheard of for us to kill people. Was your interest in me completely fake?"

"No. Get that ride. I feel like we should talk about this more at your house." Malik wasn't used to talking to a vampire about sex while walking down a sidewalk in one of Denver's most expensive neighborhoods.

"If you're okay walking, I only live a few blocks away. If you'd rather get a car, we can do that too. When I mentioned it before, I was debating about which method I preferred, but it seems to be a nice night out if you don't mind the walk."

A.J. Marcus and Caitlin Ricci

Malik decided not to remind Aren again about how he was a werewolf. He enjoyed being outside, no matter what the weather was like, as opposed to being in a cramped car. "I'd rather walk. Do you think they'll make you king now?"

Surprisingly, Aren shrugged. "Not totally sure. Aloren will probably let me know tomorrow night. Karl wasn't well liked. Geb was much better. He was fair and people enjoyed being around him. Karl had only proven himself to be an ass. Without a king, there would be some turmoil. The Vampire Council won't allow that. Too much risk of exposure, which is why it sounds like Aloren was planning on killing Karl anyway. What is your plan now?"

Malik hadn't given it a whole lot of thought. "Cheryl is all that's left of my pack. We may join another and try to find our places there. As a woman, she'll be much easier to accept than I will. We're always looking for mothers for the next generation, but other males might see me as a threat." Even if he'd only been alpha for a short while, and had gotten the position by default,

Hunted

Malik had never heard of a former alpha being accepted into a new pack.

"Do you need to have a pack?"

"Sort of. We need to have others, but I've heard of people making a pack around humans before. We can't live in solitude but, as much as it's nice to have other wolves around, that's not always the best situation for us to be in."

Aren grew silent as they crossed the street at the corner and Malik thought about what his life would be like now. So much had happened lately, he was still trying to get his feet under himself. But Cheryl was safe, and that had been his driving goal. Now he supposed finding them a place to live would be his next task. Sure, they could go back and rebuild the pack compound, but there were so many memories there, he wasn't sure either of them would be comfortable. He needed to talk to her about it. As soon as he woke up, he'd get ahold of her through Daniel or Emory, and they could work things out. If Cheryl had done the smart thing and stuck with the vampires. Otherwise, he'd have to track her down, but he was her alpha and could easily sense her no matter where she went.

They stopped in front of a small brick home, and Aren led him up the front steps. It wasn't as nice as the other houses around it, but it was still well kept and there were flowers in the yard.

"Were the snapdragons here before you moved in?" Malik asked.

"No." Aren stopped with his hand on the doorknob and looked over his shoulder at the flower bed. "I planted them. Sometimes I like to come out really late at night and sit and play with them. Have you ever done that?"

Malik chuckled. "Not since I was a kid." He followed Aren inside and was glad for the warmth. He'd expected a vampire's home to be cold, with quite a few coffins lying around. But Aren had soft leather furniture, old photographs on the wall, and chocolate mints in a dish by the front door.

Malik went to the photos. They looked like they were from different periods, and he wasn't good at guessing at clothing types, but the earliest ones had to be from the early nineteen hundreds. And every single one of them was of a house. "What's with all the houses?"

"All the places I've lived," Aren said, coming up behind him. "Ever since they invented the camera anyway. Some of us collect things during our lives to remind us of where we've been or what we've lived through. I have photographs of the places I've called home. We tend to move around, every fifteen to twenty years usually, so we see a lot of places. Someday I need to go back to all the homes I had before photography came about and get pictures of them. Some of them should still be standing. I especially liked the house I had in Spain. It was right on the Mediterranean, and every night I would go down to the beach and lay there looking up at the moon with no one else around me."

Malik turned back and smiled. "It sounds nice."

Aren slipped an arm around his waist and Malik stepped in closer to him. "Thank you for not drawing attention to yourself at the party."

"Thank you for doing what you did to help us. It couldn't have been easy." Malik kissed his cheek, and when Aren didn't pull away, he brought his lips to Aren's mouth. There was a couch nearby. Malik moved them to it and settled himself over Aren's lap. He'd been resisting the attraction he felt toward Aren, but the vampire had proven to be a friend and acted like he was interested in more. Malik wanted to find out what he was really like and was willing to take a chance.

Soon their gentle kisses turned hungry, and Malik moaned softly as Aren grabbed onto his hips, bringing them together. He tilted his head back, inviting Malik to kiss his throat and then his chest. Malik's hands shook as he worked to get Aren's shirt open. His skin was still colder than Malik was used to, but the house was warm and he didn't mind. Aren was muscular, and a light spattering of hair covered his chest and trailed down his stomach.

Malik kept his mouth against Aren's neck, gently sucking him, as he squeezed him through his pants. He was already hard, and Malik smiled as he managed to bring Aren off the couch with just his hand. It didn't make any sense how much he wanted Aren right then, but he wasn't going to question it either.

Aren went for Malik's pants.

Malik kept squeezing him, making Aren squirm as he struggled to get Malik's pants open.

"You need to stop if you want to have sex," Aren groaned.

Malik just laughed. "Maybe you should try harder. Or maybe if you'd just ask nicely for me to take my pants off..."

Aren hissed, sounding frustrated. Malik was surprised to see his fangs. He didn't want to be bitten, but he wasn't bothered by them either. He slipped off Aren's lap and undid his pants, letting them drop to his ankles. His shoes were easy to get off, and then he was standing naked in front of Aren. He let Aren look at him for a moment before he was back on the couch with him and getting Aren's pants off.

The moment his cock was free, Malik was right there, slipping his mouth over Aren's head. He bobbed his mouth quickly, loving every soft gasp and groan Aren let out as he squeezed his hand over Malik's back.

"Don't you dare make me cum," Aren grumbled.

Malik rolled his eyes. If that's what Aren wanted, then he'd hold off. He pulled away, but Aren was already desperate. He didn't have long to get himself prepared before he was back on Aren's lap, facing away from him this time. With Aren's arms around him, holding him tightly, Malik felt cared for. Aren sheathed himself inside of him, stretching Malik and making him cry out. Then Aren let him take over, allowing him to choose how Malik wanted him.

He lifted himself over Aren's cock, riding him as slowly as he could to draw out their pleasure. Malik leaned back against him, kissing Aren's cheek and mouth as Aren ran his hands over his chest. Aren's cool fingers left trails of heat where they passed over his body. Malik wanted to stretch things out—Aren was drawing something out of him, awakening feelings deep inside him. His cock was free to sway as he rode Aren.

"Tell me you love this," Malik gasped against Aren's lips.

"My cock should tell you that enough."

Hunted

Malik nipped at his chin.

"You shouldn't bite a vampire," Aren teased.

Malik laughed. "You shouldn't piss off a werewolf."

Aren wrapped his arms around Malik's chest. "I do love this. You feel amazing and I love the way your ass fits on my lap. Like you were made for me. And I love the weight of you over my thighs and the soft tickle of your hair against my face. And I especially love getting to touch you everywhere I want to when we're like this." He dipped his hands to the base of Malik's cock. And then he began to stroke him. "Are you going to cum for me, my wolf?"

Malik buried his face in Aren's neck and nodded. He was close, and so was Aren. "Stroke me fast. Tell me I'm yours."

Aren kept one hand on hip and the other clamped around his cock as he slid his hand over him. Malik's pleasure grew with each stroke of his hand. "You're my wolf, mine. I can fuck you whenever I want. However, I want to. Isn't that right? Don't you want that?"

Malik whimpered and stretched back against him, wanting him even more. He loved being possessed by someone. Aren turned and scraped his fangs over Malik's shoulder and that surprising touch, that minute bit of pain, sent him crashing over the edge. He tossed his head back and cried out in his pleasure, seconds before Aren released his cum inside of his ass.

Aren licked off his fingers while Malik hazily looked over at him. He got up, but only enough to land on the couch next to Aren, and he stayed there, naked and perfectly happy, until morning.

Malik shifted his shoulders in the borrowed shirt. It was amazing that he and Aren were the same size, at least in shirts. Before Aren had fallen asleep for the day, in a bed like a normal person but with blackout curtains to keep the sunlight from causing him problems, he'd given Malik his credit card with instructions to go shopping and get something nice for himself. They were expecting the Vampire Council that night and he had to look his best. Malik wasn't sure if his opinion of his best would match Aren's ideas.

He reached Cheryl before he set out, and by the time he'd stepped to the curb, she and Brandon were pulling up in Daniel's car.

"Daniel must not live very far away," Malik said as he opened the back seat and slid in. There was the lingering smell of sex coming from both of them.

"Not really." Cheryl steered the car down the street. "Plus, it helps that we're in a city I at least know a little bit of. According to Emory, a lot of the lower level vampires are fanned out around the master covenstead. They try to stay close in case the court needs things."

Having had a pack compound, Malik understood the idea of keeping everyone close by. "Makes sense."

"Thank you for freeing me from Felicia," Brandon said with a heavy European accent. "I've been looking for a way to get away from her for some time now."

'I thought from what Aloren said last night that European vampires were changing their tune about shifters." Malik wished there wasn't so much new stuff flying at him all at once. He was a new alpha, he had a potential new lover, and was expected to understand how the supernatural community in other countries worked when he barely understood how the one in America did.

"The Vampire Council has issued some new decrees about treating all of us like equal species, but it's not catching on with all the vampires. Some like the old ways. Felicia isn't as bad as some, but she likes brawny guys on her arm."

Cheryl stopped for a red light and giggled as she patted Brandon's leg. "I happen to like hunky guys on my arm too."

"And your arm is a lot more pleasurable than hers, as are your thighs, your breasts-"

Malik cleared his throat. "Hey, we're supposed to be shopping here."

"Oh yeah." Cheryl hit the accelerator as the light changed. "Where to, Cherry Creek or 16th Street?"

"Aren said he and I need to expect to attend the Vampire Council tonight and to look nice." Malik hoped Cheryl would be

Hunted

able to help him find something suitable.

"Your idea of nice or his?" Cheryl turned to the left.

"If you are undecided, I think I can help," Brandon said, turning to look at Malik over the back seat. "Yes, I think I can see some things we need to do."

Inwardly, Malik groaned. He hadn't planned on the bear playing dress up with him. Having Cheryl do it would be bad enough. He wondered if his life would just be easier walking into the Council meeting and offering himself up as a late-night snack.

"So we're going to wait and see what options we're offered?" Malik asked as they drove back toward Aren's house. It had been a long day—he had new clothes and freshly trimmed hair. While they'd been shopping, using Aren's credit card, they'd discussed what they wanted to do.

Apparently, Cheryl and Brandon had hit it off really well. Brandon had asked to join their pack and Cheryl had offered to sponsor him if Malik wanted to go that route and not just accept him in instantly. Having another pack member made Malik happy, and he'd agreed. They'd even taken the time to stop in one of the more reclusive parks so they could be alone long enough for Brandon to pledge himself to Malik and Cheryl. They'd all exchanged a bit of blood to seal their pack bond, and afterward, Malik felt more powerful than ever. He was finally a true alpha, and it wasn't scaring him as much as the idea of it had a few days earlier.

"See what Aren has to offer you, and what Aloren has in mind for everyone, then we'll make our final decisions." Cheryl pulled onto Aren's street. "It's more than a little scary that we're the only werewolves in half a continent."

"I really doubt the vampires were that successful in trying to wipe us out," Malik said. "But it may take a bit to hunt everyone up."

"At least we're not going to have the vampires breathing down our necks while we do it," Cheryl said.

"Unless we want them to," Malik said. He liked having Aren breathing on the back of his neck. It was hot and sexy.

Hunted

Cheryl pulled up in front of Aren's house. "Yeah, unless you want Aren to." She turned off the car and moved so she could see into the back seat. "You're okay going into that meeting without us?"

Although he wanted Cheryl with him as a show of pack solidarity, he knew Lady Felicia would be there and he didn't want to be accused of stealing her bear the same night that Aren spoke to the Council about killing Karl. Since Lady Felicia was a member of the Council, that might complicate things. Better that she just thinks he ran off, as long as she didn't decide to hunt him down. "Aren will be with me. I don't doubt that he has my best interests at heart."

"Okay." She reached out to give him an awkward hug. "If you need us, call. We'll come running and the vampires won't know what hit them."

He chuckled softly. "I'm sure they won't."

Feeling better than he had since the night everything went to hell, Malik got out of the car and headed into Aren's house. The sun was just dropping below Mt. Evans as he opened the door and went in to wait for Aren to wake up and greet the night.

Hunted

Chapter Twelve

Aren had debated making Malik wear the collar again. With it on, Malik would be viewed as Aren's plaything and would be safe from the other vampires. Without it, Malik would be more of an equal and would have to stand on his own merits. They had a quick discussion about it before Aloren called and informed Aren he had thirty minutes to get to the covenstead.

Malik looked impressive in the expensive suit he'd bought, and Aren had to approve of how the suit fit like it had been tailored when they hadn't had time for that. He adjusted the shirt's collar, then rubbed his hand down the opening, enjoying the warmth of Malik's skin against his palm and the way the hair on Malik's chest played across his fingers.

"We don't have time for that," Malik said before giving him a quick kiss.

"I know." Aren sighed and stepped back from Malik. The werewolf was warm, and he liked the warmth. "We need to get going.

Daniel will be here to drive us over in a moment."

There was a knock on the door.

"Or sooner." Aren walked to the door.

Daniel and Emory looked dressed to the nines as they stood there on Aren's porch.

"You two prepping for a show or something?" Aren asked as he gestured for them all to head for the car.

"We're going to show solidarity with you and figured we should make a good impression. We talked with some of the other vampires in town and most everyone except Raul is going to stand with you. You're going to make a great king." Daniel opened the back door of the car, looking a lot like a footman.

"We don't know if they're even going to offer me a kingship," Aren said, doing his best to not show his nervousness or his reluctance to take the position. But he didn't know of any other vampires who were suited for the position.

Emory huffed. "Who else would take the position?"

"There are lots of ambitious vampires

out there," Aren said as he settled into the seat and Daniel closed the door. He didn't bother raising his voice, well aware of the sensitivity of vampire hearing.

"But you'll be the one who can end the war on the werewolves," Malik slid across the seat and settled against Aren's side. He was a secure comfort there.

"Others could do that, particularly when Aloren announces that Karl's death was due to his hunting of your people. With such a decree from the Council, no one will think of ever doing such wholesale slaughter again." Aren hoped he was right. So much of what vampires did, they did on whim. That made them dangerous, even to their own kind.

"I guess we'll see what's going to happen when we get there," Daniel said as he started the car.

Richard, the gateman, waved them through when they pulled up. He didn't even make them roll down the window for his personal inspection. Aren wasn't sure when the last time was he'd seen security so lax, but since Geb had been killed, Karl had been extremely paranoid that the wolves were going to charge in and kill him. Glancing to his right, Aren smiled. With Karl dead, the wolves were just waltzing into the covenstead, but Malik wasn't intent on killing anyone, not anymore.

As they entered the house, a thrall bowed to them. "Lord Aren, Lord Aloren would like you to attend him in the study. He says you can bring your wolf, but no others."

Daniel bristled beside Aren. "We're standing with him."

Aren put his hand on Daniel's arm. "I'm safe with Aloren. Don't worry about it. I can hear people gathered in the great hall. Sounds like dinner time. Go get a drink and we'll join you shortly." He'd never had people who wanted to follow him before. Daniel and Emory's devotion made him smile and warmed his heart almost as much as Malik's steady presence at his side.

"Come on." He took Malik's hand and led the way to the study. There were butterflies ravaging his stomach, but he didn't want to show it to anyone. He had no doubt that his destiny was going to be decided in the next few minutes if it hadn't been already.

The thick mahogany door of the study stood open. Aren paused for a moment. He looked at Malik, who gave him a tight smile and a reassuring nod. Even if he hadn't known Malik very long, there was something special in that look. Aren knew Malik would stand by him.

"You don't have to knock," Aloren said from within. "This isn't even my study. I'm just borrowing it."

Feeling stupid for stopping, Aren continued into the room.

Aloren stood at the bookshelves to their right. "You know, I can tell Karl didn't have the time or didn't bother getting this library set up with his books. These ancient texts are much more Geb than Karl."

"I know. Honestly, I don't think Karl spent much time reading," Aren said as he stopped in the middle of the room.

"Probably not. He was more of a carnal pleasures sort of man." Aloren put the book in his hand back on the shelf and turned toward Aren. "If Geb hadn't been his sire, he never would've lasted as long as he did. If you had stepped up and fought him for his position, you could've had all of this months ago."

Aren shook his head. "I didn't want it then. Honestly, I don't know if I want it now."

Aloren shrugged. "Now you have no choice. We need a strong and level hand here in the colonies. I've been in contact with the rest of the Council. We all approve of you becoming king. Honestly, I'm relieved you're here. I wasn't looking forward to seeking out a proper candidate."

"I don't really get an option, do I?" Aren had been in the circle of power long enough to know the answer, but he had to ask it.

"No." Aloren closed the distance between them with almost human slowness. "Of the other vampires I knew here in the colonies, most of them would be little better than Karl, although, with his death as an example, they might be on their best behavior when they thought we were looking."

"But you're always looking." Aren knew the Council had eyes in every court across the world. There was very little that happened that they didn't know about.

Aloren chuckled. "And that's why you'll make a good leader, and a member of the Council."

Aren took two steps back and brought his hands up. "Now wait a minute."

"No." Aloren cut him off. "One of the things the Council decided a few weeks ago was that all the kings and queens around the world would have new seats on the Council. We're trying to integrate everything. In case you didn't notice, the world is getting smaller and we need to all work together. That means those of us in power working as one. That will also help prevent things like Karl from happening again. If Geb had been a Council member, we would've sent an investigative team to look into his death and wouldn't have allowed the slaughter that took place afterward."

"Would that team have included any shifters?" Malik spoke up for the first time since entering the house.

Aloren turned his attention to Malik and Aren wished he'd just stayed quiet.

"Actually, it would have."

"Then you would've known it wasn't a werewolf around the spot where Geb was killed, but a oneform wolf," Malik continued. "The smell is subtly different. I'm not surprised your people missed it, but a shifter would know the difference."

"And that is why we're trying to work closer with the shifter community in Europe." Aloren gave them both a smile. "There's so many little things that we miss from time to time. We might be old and think we know everything, but in truth, we don't. I'm hoping the two of you can help unite the vampire and shifter community here in the colonies. Actually, once I'm done here, I get to go to South America and speak with Queen Aleta Montoya to try to get her on board with the changes."

"I've heard tale she's a bit of a traditionalist," Aren said.

"So have I," Aloren agreed. "But in the technological age we live in, it's time we all start changing."

Aren nodded.

"What are you going to want from us?"

Hunted

Malik asked.

Squeezing his hand a little harder than necessary, Aren really hoped he'd be quiet and stop drawing Aloren's attention. Although so far, Aloren was treating him more or less as an equal, which was surprising.

"I want you, as wolf king, and Aren as vampire king, to join the two communities together. The risk of discovery by humans grows greater every day. We have to work as one to make sure we can stay safely in the shadows."

Malik shook his head. "But we don't have a wolf king. We run as packs and each pack answers only to itself."

"And that needs to change. If you hadn't all be operating independently, Karl's attacks wouldn't have been so complete and devastating." Aloren paced a little bit. "You might see about getting the shifter community around you too. Everything you can do to help with supernatural unity will be a good thing."

"Bringing people together." Malik nodded slowly. "It's going to be a big job."

"And I think you two are the perfect ones to do it." Aloren stepped closer and put his hands on both their shoulder. "So what do you say? Kings?"

Aren looked into Malik's green eyes. They were wide and curious about what was going to happen. Malik nodded. Aren smiled, then turned to Aloren. "Kings."

"Kings," Malik repeated.

"Good. Now let's go announce things to the assembled vampires. You're both going to need to have good people around you to help you pull this off. Start thinking about who you trust." Aloren looped his arms in theirs and led them out of the room.

The nervousness in Aren's stomach increased, but he fought it down. His long life was changing, but he'd deal with it. He didn't have much choice, but at least he had Malik at his side through it. The werewolf was powerful and sexy. They were going to make a great team, and together he didn't doubt they'd be able to overcome whatever hurdles the supernatural world threw at them.

He leaned back and looked around Aloren's head and caught Malik doing the

same. "Thank you," he silently mouthed.
Malik smiled and blew him a kiss.

The End

To keep up with the latest from

Mystichawker Press, read our newsletter:

Signup available at

www.mystichawkerpress.com

A.J. Marcus and Caitlin Ricci

About the Authors

Caitlin Ricci was fortunate growing up to be surrounded by family and teachers that encouraged her love of reading. She has always been a voracious reader and that love of the written word easily morphed into a passion for writing. She comes from a military family and the men and women of the armed forces are close to her heart. She also enjoys gardening and horseback riding in the Colorado Rockies where she calls home with her wonderful husband and their two dogs. Her belief that there is no one true path to happily ever after runs deeply through all of her stories.

www.CaitlinRicci.com
authorcaitlinricci@gmail.com

A.J. Marcus has been writing to pass the time since high school. The stories he wrote helped him deal with life. A few years ago, he started sharing those stories with friends who enjoyed them, and he has started sending his works out into the world to share with other people. He lives in the mountains with his extremely supportive husband. They have a lot of critters, including dogs, cats, birds, horses, and rabbits. When not writing, A.J. spends a lot of time hiking, trail riding, or just driving in the mountains. Nature provides a lot of inspiration for his work and keeps him writing. He is also an avid photographer and

Hunted

falconer. Don't get him started talking about his birds because he won't stop for a while.

Web Contact Info:
Website: www.ajmarcus.com
Email: andy@ajmarcus.com
Twitter: twitter.com/#!/aj_marcus
Facebook: http://
www.facebook.com/authorajmarcus

Other Books by Caitlin Ricci

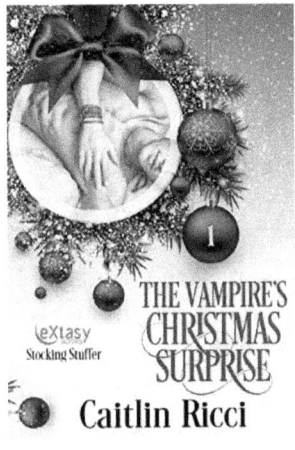

The last thing Armand expected to find out by his woodpile was a werewolf. The man is freezing, injured, and in desperate need of some help. But for vampires and werewolves, centuries of old conflicts make being friends now nearly impossible. One night of comfort by the fire might be enough to sway a chilly heart if both Armand and Puck are willing to take that chance.

Available from Extasy Books.

Wherever Ebooks are sold

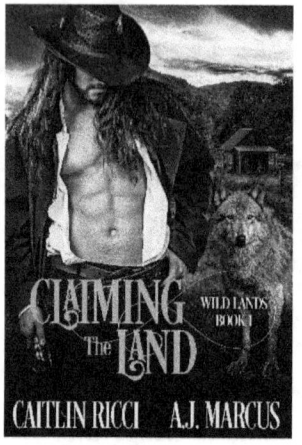

Elijah Abbey and his family have claimed a large tract of land that will one day become part of Colorado. They have all the room they could ever want to start the cattle ranch of their dreams. But someone else says they have a right to the same spot, and he's not willing to go away quietly.

The land is also the ancestral home of a group of werewolves. With two groups of humans closing in on their territory, the wolves quickly realize that a compromise has to be made. One group of humans leaves them alone, but the other has only shown them violence.

Also Available from A.J. Marcus

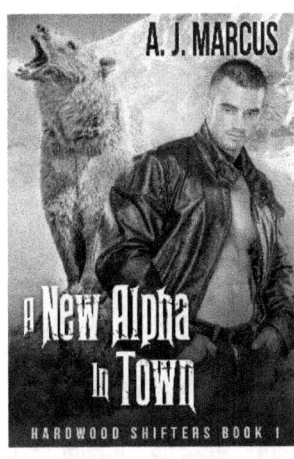

The past year has been hard for werewolf Tanner Groff. After his pack was killed by shifter hunters, he's staying on the move, looking to warn other shifters there's a band of militaristic hunters looking to kill every shifter they can find. When he catches the scent of a bear shifter named Van, Tanner changes his course and follows in hopes of having a quiet discussion with Van. But before that can happen, the hunters strike sending them on a desperate rescue mission they aren't sure will succeed. Being in close quarters with passions running high, Tanner and Van find a mutual attraction and hope they can survive long enough to explore it and the new path their lives are taking.

Available from Extasy Books.

Wherever Ebooks are sold

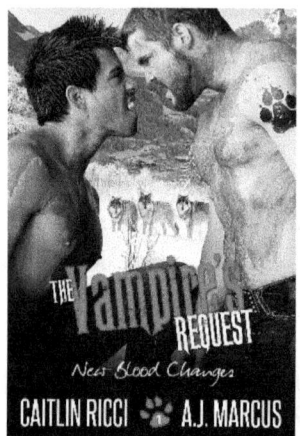

Jason Blue is a new alpha and still trying to figure out how to run his pack. One thing he knows beyond a shadow of a doubt is vampires and litches are a bad thing, and he wants nothing to do with them, particularly after the litch who's trying to control the local vampires killed the previous alpha pair of the Sky Ridge pack. When he finds vampires fighting in his territory he does the only thing he can, help kill the aggressors. But he's unprepared for a request for sanctuary.

Saul Ledo chafes under the tight, unchanging hold the litches have on the vampires. Like a good number of the younger vampires, he's ready for a change, even if that means taking on the rulers who've controlled his people for thousands of years. The problem is he's going to need help. Running out of choices, he finds hope of getting out from under the litches once and for all when he meets Jason.

Available from Extasy Books.

Wherever Ebooks are sold